MOUSE IN THE MISTLETOE

'It's definitely sleet,' James remarked, stretching out a gloved hand to try and catch some. 'But let's hope it'll turn to snow for Christmas.'

'Oh yes, I really hope so,' said Mandy. She longed to get her sledge out again and go sliding down from the Beacon to the bottom of the hill. Thoughts of such energetic activity brought Muffin back to her mind. 'Aren't you surprised how lively Muffin is all of a sudden?' she asked James.

'A bit,' he said. 'But better that than a dead mouse.'

Mandy smiled. 'Seriously, James, I think it's odd that she's changed so much. I mean, how can a mouse take on a whole new personality after a few days?' she asked, remembering what her father had told her about mouse behaviour.

'I don't know,' said James, jumping over a huge puddle on the pavement. 'Maybe she's just glad to be back home.'

Animal Ark series

Rachael Ewing

LUCY DANIELS

Mouse
— in the —
Mistletoe

Illustrations by Ann Baum

*Hodder
Children's
Books*

a division of Hodder Headline

Special thanks to Andrea Abbott.
Thanks also to C. J. Hall, B.Vet.Med., M.R.C.V.S., for reviewing
the veterinary information contained in this book.

First published in Great Britain in 2000
by Hodder Children's Books

For more information about Animal Ark,
please contact www.animalark.co.uk

10 9 8 7 6 5 4 3 2 1

A Catalogue record for this book is available from the British Library.

ISBN 0 340 77877 6

Typeset by Avon Dataset Ltd, Bidford-on-Avon, Warks

Printed and bound in Great Britain by
Clays Ltd, St Ives plc

Hodder Children's Books
A Division of Hodder Headline Limited
338 Euston Road
London NW1 3BH

One

'What's in there, Mandy?' asked her father, Adam Hope. He was pointing to a plastic lunch box that Mandy had popped on the kitchen table before hurriedly pouring herself a bowlful of muesli.

'Oh, just some hazelnuts and fishy niblets I bought at the supermarket on Saturday,' Mandy said, tucking into her breakfast.

'Funny sort of lunch – especially the fishy things. I thought you were a vegetarian,' teased Mr Hope, who stood drinking a cup of tea and warming himself next to the Aga.

'Very funny, Dad,' laughed Mandy. 'They're for Sammy and Tiddles.'

'Ernie's cat and pet squirrel?' asked Mandy's mum, Emily, looking up from the newspaper that she was quickly scanning before the start of morning surgery.

The Hopes knew most of the animals in and around the Yorkshire village of Welford, where they lived. This was because Mandy's parents were vets, and over the years they had treated nearly all of the local pets and farm animals, and even some of the wildlife from the surrounding moors and forests. Their surgery, Animal Ark, was attached to the back of their home – which was why Mandy was able to get to know and even sometimes help with the animals that were brought there.

'That's right, Mum,' said Mandy. 'I thought that James and I could—' A loud thud in the hallway interrupted Mandy.

'That sounds like a lot of post!' she exclaimed. She pushed her chair back from the old pine table and dashed out of the kitchen. A big pile of envelopes lay on the front doormat. Mandy gathered it up and began shuffling through it on her way back to the warm kitchen.

'Anything interesting?' asked Mr Hope, rinsing the breakfast dishes in the sink.

'Yes – one for me,' replied Mandy, tearing open a large envelope. 'And it looks like James's writing.'

Mandy pulled out a card bearing a picture of a black Labrador wearing a Santa hat. The words 'Woofing you a Merry Christmas' appeared in a speech bubble near the dog's mouth.

'This can *only* be from James.' Mandy smiled. She opened the card to read the message inside.

'Why do you say that?' asked Mrs Hope.

'Who else would make a Christmas card for me on a computer and put a picture of his own dog on the front?' said Mandy, chuckling.

James Hunter was her best friend, and his dog, Blackie, was one of the nicest dogs Mandy knew – as well as probably the most disobedient!

'"Dear Mandy," ' she read aloud. '"Can't wait to start the Christmas visits on Monday afternoon. From James and Blackie."'

'Christmas visits?' Mr Hope asked, frowning.

'Yes, I was just going to tell you about them when the post came,' said Mandy. She went on to explain that she and James were going to visit all the old people in Welford that had pets so that they could make sure they were all OK and wish them a happy Christmas. 'We're starting today after school,' she said, putting the plastic lunch box in her bag.

'Ah – that explains the nuts and niblets for Sammy and Tiddles. You're going round to Ernie Bell's cottage and giving his pets a treat this afternoon,' said Mr Hope.

Mandy nodded as she pulled on her jacket. Smiling broadly, Mrs Hope got up from the table and gave her a quick hug, saying, 'I should have guessed you'd think of something special for all your animal friends at Christmas-time.'

More than anything else, Mandy loved animals – all animals – and she knew exactly what she was going to be when she grew up – a vet, just like her mum and dad.

As Mandy swung her bag on to her shoulder, the phone rang. 'I'll get it,' she said, dashing back into the hall and picking up the receiver. 'Welford 703267.' Mandy listened intently for a moment then said, 'You need to speak to my mum or dad. Hold on a minute. Mum,' she called, 'Mr

Grimshaw's worried about Biddy – she hurt herself chasing through Lamb's Wood yesterday and is having trouble standing up. He thinks you might have to take a look at her.'

Mandy waited apprehensively while Emily Hope spoke to Robbie Grimshaw. She remembered the first time she and James had met the old man and his Welsh collie, Biddy. They had gone to ask him for help in rescuing a colony of rabbits that a wealthy farmer, Sam Western, wanted to shoot. Robbie lived in a weathered old cottage on a smallholding, down a neglected and bumpy lane in Lamb's Wood, up past Woodbridge Farm Park.

'I think it's best,' Mrs Hope was saying, 'if I come up after morning surgery. I'll examine her and, if necessary, bring her back here in the Land-rover.' She hung up and turned to Mandy. 'Looks like we may have a new patient for a few days.'

Mandy was about to ask for more details when she glanced at her watch. 'I'd better get going!' she cried. 'Or I'll miss the bus!' She sped out of the door and found herself slipping and skidding as she ran along the ice-covered lane to the crossroads outside the Fox and Goose.

* * *

After school that afternoon, when the bus dropped Mandy and James off at the village green, Mandy was the first to notice that the Christmas tree outside the pub had been decorated. 'Wow, look at that!' she cried excitedly.

'It's great!' exclaimed James. They stood for a moment gazing at the tall tree with its twinkling lights and myriad sparkling decorations.

'Now it *really* feels like Christmas is nearly here,' Mandy said, as they crossed the road and headed for Ernie Bell's tiny cottage, which stood in a row of five next to the pub.

'It's already come for Sara Bailey,' remarked James. Sara, like James, was eleven and in the year below Mandy at school.

'How come?' asked Mandy, turning down the pathway to the row of small cottages.

'She told us in class today that she's had her Christmas present already,' explained James. 'It's a black-eyed white mouse.'

'A mouse! Isn't she lucky? Did you see it?' asked Mandy, stopping in front of one of the entrance gates.

'No,' replied James. 'Sara said it's too cold to bring her out. Oh, and she's called Muffin.'

'Cute name,' said Mandy. She knocked on the door of the ramshackle little house.

'Who is it?' called a gruff voice from inside.

'Mandy and James,' replied Mandy.

'Just a minute,' said the man's voice.

After a moment, the battered old door creaked open and Ernie Bell appeared on the doorstep. He peered at them from under his bushy white eyebrows. 'What can I do for you two?' he asked in his throaty voice.

'We've come to wish you and Sammy and Tiddles a happy Christmas,' said Mandy.

'And we've brought something for the three of you,' added James, searching round in his school bag and bringing out an envelope.

'Well, you'd better come in out of the cold,' said Ernie. He ushered them into his neat little sitting-room.

'Hello, Tiddles,' said Mandy, to a pretty grey kitten curled up on a well-worn armchair in front of the fire. Hearing her name, Tiddles turned on to her back and stretched her little body to its full length, then stood up and rubbed herself along Mandy's outstretched hand.

'You know I've brought you something tasty,

don't you?' Mandy said with a chuckle, smoothing the cat's fur with one hand and reaching into her school-bag with the other.

'Aye, she can always sniff out food, that one,' agreed Ernie, a hint of tenderness in his voice.

Mandy pulled out the plastic box containing the fish niblets and gave a handful to Tiddles. The kitten munched eagerly on the treats.

'How's Sammy?' asked James.

'Just champion, lad. Would you like to see him?' said Ernie.

'Yes, please,' said Mandy quickly. 'We've got some hazelnuts for him.'

Ernie led the way out to the backyard, where Sammy, his pet squirrel, was housed in a timber-and-wire mesh run. Hearing the arrival of his owner, Sammy scampered over to the fence. Mandy and James pushed some nuts through the mesh. The squirrel grabbed one, then, sitting on his haunches and holding the nut in his little paws, gnawed vigorously on his Christmas treat. He stopped briefly to look directly at Mandy and James, then hastily resumed his feasting.

'Do you think he was thanking us?' said James, laughing.

'Could be,' said Ernie. 'Now, how about a drink?'

The two friends nodded and followed Ernie back into the warmth of the cottage, where the old man set about making a pot of tea and pouring out some lemonade.

'This is for you, Mr Bell,' said James, handing an envelope to Ernie once they were sitting round the fire with their drinks. 'I made it myself – on my computer.'

'You young 'uns are clever with all this technical stuff these days,' said Ernie, pulling a Christmas card out of the envelope. The picture on the front of the card was of a nativity scene and one of the animals standing by the crib was Blackie! 'Well, I've never seen one like that before!' said Mr Bell with a wry smile. 'What's not changed, though, is the crib. It looks just like the one in the nativity scene in our church.'

'It should,' said James. 'I drew a copy of it, then scanned that on to my computer.'

'Oh, I see,' replied Mr Bell, sounding as if he didn't see at all! 'Anyway, the thing is, I made that crib myself.'

'Did you?' asked Mandy with interest. She knew Mr Bell was a retired carpenter, but had never imagined he was responsible for the sturdy little crib that had graced the church at Christmas-time ever since she could remember.

'Aye, lass. Years ago, the vicar at the time asked me to make it. He liked the idea of the village carpenter making a crib for a baby that grew up to be a carpenter himself!' said Ernie softly.

'That means you're a big part of Christmas in Welford,' said Mandy enthusiastically. She sprinkled some more niblets on the floor for Tiddles, who'd been rubbing herself against

Mandy's legs in the hope of earning more treats. '*And* you ring the church bells on Christmas Day. That must be really special.'

'Not really,' said Ernie gruffly. 'Bell-ringing on Christmas Day is no different from doing it on other days.'

'But Christmas *is* special,' protested Mandy.

'That it might be for you young 'uns, but it's not for the likes of me. I'm too old for it now. It's just too much trouble,' insisted Ernie, as he poured himself a second cup of tea.

A little while later, as Mandy and James were about to go their separate ways at the crossroads, Mandy turned to James. 'Mr Bell seemed a bit down in the dumps. Imagine not liking Christmas!'

'He's usually a bit grumpy,' said James. 'Perhaps he'll cheer up as it gets closer.'

'Let's hope so,' said Mandy, turning for home. 'Oh, I've just remembered,' she called over her shoulder, as she ran down the lane towards Animal Ark. 'We might have a new patient at the surgery – Robbie Grimshaw's collie – I'll let you know in the morning.'

Reaching home, Mandy bounded up the steps

and through the glass doors leading into Animal Ark.

'What's the hurry?' asked the receptionist, Jean Knox, looking over the top of her spectacles, as Mandy burst into the waiting-room.

'Is Biddy here?' Mandy asked, breathlessly. But instead of waiting for a reply, she dashed through to the residential unit to find out for herself.

In the residential unit, Mandy scanned the rows of cages used for animals who required on-going treatment or were recovering from surgery. Only a few of the cages were occupied today. In one, there was a small fluffy dog who was being treated for an infected wound on his paw, while another cage held a black rabbit with a torn ear. Mandy stopped and petted the dog and rabbit who seemed to perk up when they saw her.

The animals in the residential unit always recognised her, because whenever she had the time she helped out at Animal Ark, where her duties included feeding the resident patients and cleaning out their cages.

'How's your paw today?' Mandy said, crouching down in front of the little dog and scratching him gently behind one ear. As she spoke, a short bark erupted from one of the larger cages further down the row.

'Is that you, Biddy?' asked Mandy. She straightened up and went to investigate who was in the cage.

A black-and-white Welsh collie lay on the soft bedding. She wagged her tail slowly when Mandy appeared, but made no attempt to get up.

'It *is* you, Biddy!' said Mandy quietly, reaching her hand through the cage and massaging the dog's neck lightly. Robbie Grimshaw had said on the phone that morning that Biddy was injured, so Mandy knew she must keep the dog quiet and still. 'What have you done to yourself?' she said, soothingly.

'Strained her back severely,' said a voice right next to Mandy.

Mandy jumped. 'Mum – I didn't hear you come in!'

Mrs Hope smiled. Bending down to kiss Mandy on her cheek, she asked, 'Had a good day at school?'

'Mmm – not too bad,' murmured Mandy. 'But what about Biddy? What treatment is she having?'

'A short course of acupuncture should do the trick,' her mother told her. Mrs Hope had studied acupuncture while in China, and often treated injured or arthritic animals in this way. 'I'll need to do the procedure every other day, so she'll probably be with us for about ten days,' Mrs Hope explained. 'Now,' she said, walking towards the door, 'I must get back to work. There's a waiting-room full of patients.'

'Robbie's going to miss her,' Mandy commented, following her mother out of the residential unit.

'Mmm, but he will be visiting her,' said Mrs Hope, opening the door to the consulting room. 'In fact, he said he'd be here about now.'

Mandy went into the waiting-room and saw that Robbie had arrived. She thought he looked very anxious, so she went over to talk to him. 'I'll take you in to see Biddy, if you like,' she offered. 'I've just been with her and she looks quite comfortable. Don't worry – Mum will soon have her as right as rain and then she'll be home in time for Christmas.'

Robbie tugged at his grey beard. 'As long as she gets better – that's all that counts. It doesn't matter whether she's home by Christmas or not.'

'But it wouldn't be the same for you if she wasn't,' protested Mandy, leading the way to the residential unit.

'The same as what?' asked Robbie gruffly. 'Christmas is just another day after all.'

After Robbie had seen Biddy, Mandy stood at the glass doors watching him cycle off on his rusty old bike. She sighed and shook her head.

'What's the matter?' inquired Jean, looking up from the computer screen.

'I'm not sure,' said Mandy, puzzled. 'You see, both Ernie and Robbie seem quite miserable and don't even want to celebrate Christmas. I just don't understand it. How can *anyone* not be excited at this time of the year?'

Two

The next day's visit was to Mrs McFarlane, who ran the village post office. She had a green budgie called Billy, so this time Mandy took along a packet of birdseed. James's computer-generated card bore a picture of a postman carrying a very heavy bag of mail and being chased by Blackie with a Christmas cracker in his mouth!

Mrs McFarlane was pleased to see them and laughed when she saw the Christmas card, but she was very busy sorting out all the extra Christmas post and couldn't spare the time to sit and talk to Mandy and James.

'That's what Christmas does to you,' the postmistress complained wearily, brushing a strand of grey hair off her forehead. 'Wears you out with heaps of extra work.'

'But Christmas is fantastic!' protested James.

'Maybe it is for you youngsters. But I don't think I'll even bother to get a tree in this year,' said Mrs McFarlane. She turned her attention back to a huge pile of envelopes and parcels. 'Anyway, thanks for stopping by, and thanks, too, for Billy's seed. He'll enjoy that. I'd like to chat but I must get on now, otherwise I'll be at it till late tonight.'

Outside the post office, Mandy turned to James. 'They're all the same,' she lamented, setting off at a brisk pace in the direction of Animal Ark.

'Who are?' asked James, catching up with her. He was going back to Animal Ark with Mandy for supper so that he could see Biddy. Like Mandy, James was mad about animals and loved meeting the patients that came to the surgery.

'Ernie, Robbie and now Mrs McFarlane,' she explained. 'They're all saying the same thing – that they can't be bothered with Christmas. And I thought they'd be really cheerful – especially when we went to wish them and their pets a happy Christmas.'

'So did I,' agreed James. 'Uh-oh – here comes the rain,' he said, breaking into a run.

'Wish we had our bikes!' cried Mandy, running alongside him and tugging at the hood on her anorak.

They sprinted into the lane leading to Animal Ark and almost collided with Robbie Grimshaw who was rattling along on his bike from the opposite direction.

'Been to see Biddy?' Mandy called.

'Aye,' said Robbie, skidding to a screeching halt.

'How is she?' asked James.

'Much the same,' Robbie muttered grimly. Then without another word, he pushed down on his squeaking pedals and continued on his way.

'And *he's* much the same, too,' commented Mandy as they watched Robbie disappear round the corner. 'Still miserable!'

Within a few minutes, Mandy and James had reached the Hopes' stone cottage. After pulling off their dripping anoraks in the porch and wiping the mud off their shoes, they went into the cosy kitchen where Mr Hope had the kettle on and was putting out some mince pies on a plate.

'Hello, there,' he said. 'Just in time for a snack. Care to join us? Mum will be through in a minute – she's just finishing Biddy's first course of acupuncture.'

'Ooh, yes please,' said James readily, his eyes fixed firmly on the mince-pies.

Mandy put her hands on her hips and glared at James. 'I thought you were keen to see Biddy,' she said in a mocking tone.

'I am,' said James. 'It's just that—'

'I know.' Mandy laughed. 'You're starving! But don't forget that you promised to help me clean out Biddy's cage,' she said, dumping her bag in a corner.

'You won't have to do that today,' said Mrs Hope, coming into the kitchen at that moment. She went over to the sink to wash her hands and explained that Simon, the practice nurse, had sorted out the cage while Biddy was having her acupuncture. 'You can go and see her in a while,' said Mandy's mum. 'But I think she'd probably appreciate being left alone for half an hour or so.'

Mr Hope gave James an exaggerated wink. 'You win, James! Food first, no chores, only a bit of light visiting. That's the way, lad.'

'Dad!' exclaimed Mandy, pretending to be outraged 'You're a terrible chauvinist!'

'Ah, the English scholar,' chuckled Mr Hope. 'Always has the right word for everything!'

They all sat round the table enjoying the afternoon snack and discussing the events of the day.

'How was your visit to Mrs McFarlane?' asked Mrs Hope, tucking a few unruly strands of her long red hair behind her ears.

Mandy related the details of their visit and finished off by saying how uninterested in Christmas the postmistress seemed. 'Just like Ernie and Robbie,' she complained. 'They all say they're too old and can't be bothered to celebrate. I wish there was something we could do to cheer them all up and put them in a festive mood.'

'There probably is something,' said Mrs Hope, collecting the plates and cups and putting them in the sink, 'and I have no doubt that you'll think of it.' Then she turned to Mr Hope, who was on the point of pouring out another cup of tea. 'Ready to get back to work, Adam?' she asked.

Mr Hope scrambled to his feet and made for

the doorway where he stopped, turned round and woefully said, 'Sometimes you just have to admit defeat,' but at the same time winked at James again.

While Mandy and James did the washing-up, they talked about the problem of the old people not looking forward to Christmas.

'Mum's right, you know. There *must* be something we can do to make Christmas fun for them,' said Mandy, scraping the crumbs from the mince-pies into a saucer. She opened the back door and went out to sprinkle the crumbs on the lawn. In an instant, several blackbirds gathered and began to peck lustily at the tasty scraps.

'Looks like they're having a party,' chuckled James as Mandy came back into the kitchen.

'Party! That's it!' cried Mandy, clicking her fingers. 'What a brilliant idea, James.'

James looked baffled. He took the saucer from Mandy and washed it. 'What are you talking about? I haven't had any ideas.'

'But you've given me one. We can organise a get-together for the old people and their pets!' Mandy told him. She picked up a tea towel and began to dry the dishes.

'What kind of get-together?' asked James, drying his hands on a corner of Mandy's tea towel.

'A Christmas party!' said Mandy enthusiastically.

'But they don't want to do anything for Christmas, Mandy – they've made that clear,' said James. 'How would we ever get them to come to a party?'

'Well, we'll just have to work something out,' said Mandy firmly, as she put away the last of the dishes. 'Let's go and see Biddy now.'

James followed Mandy into the residential unit, where Biddy was resting peacefully. The black-and-white Welsh collie opened her big brown eyes and gazed at them. Then, recognising Mandy, the dog began to wag her tail so vigorously that it thumped against the side of the cage.

'I think you're looking better already,' Mandy said in a soothing tone.

James patted the top of the dog's head. 'Bet you can't wait to get back to the woods,' he said. The dog wagged her tail faster and whined a little.

Mandy stood up. 'You're not to get yourself excited, Biddy,' she said. 'We'd better leave you to rest, now, but I'll come and check on you later.'

The two friends were walking away from Biddy

when Mandy suddenly stopped in her tracks. 'I've got it!' she cried. 'I know how we can get everyone to come to a party.'

'How?' asked James.

'Check-ups! Mum and Dad can give free check-ups to the pets of all the old people, and afterwards we'll throw a surprise party for them.' Mandy explained.

'That's a brilliant idea!' said James at the top of his voice.

Hearing the excitement, Biddy started to whine again. 'Oops,' whispered James sheepishly, 'we'd better talk about this somewhere else.'

They hurried back into the kitchen and started making plans for the party. James sat at the table making notes while Mandy began to get supper ready for when her parents finished evening surgery.

'It would be nice if we can give the pets a present each,' suggested James, 'but I don't think I've got enough money to buy something for all of them.'

'What about asking our friends at school to help out?' asked Mandy, scrubbing four potatoes at the sink.

'Mmm, jacket potatoes – my favourite,' said

James, as Mandy popped the potatoes into the oven.

'I know. But forget about your stomach for a minute, James, and concentrate on the party,' grinned Mandy. 'Let's ask everyone in our classes each to buy one pet a Christmas present. We could have a sort of pets lucky dip at school.'

'How would that work?' asked James, looking puzzled.

Mandy took a large block of cheese out of the fridge and began to grate it into a dish. 'Well, everyone could draw the name of an old person's pet out of a hat and then buy a present for that animal,' she explained.

'Your *third* great idea of the day. I'll have to call you Einstein soon!' said James with a laugh, sneaking a few morsels of cheese that had landed outside the dish.

Mandy tapped James's hand lightly. 'James Hunter!' she said sternly. 'Wait until suppertime.'

By the time Mr and Mrs Hope came in from the surgery, Mandy and James had finalised their plans. The party was to take place in the village hall the following Friday afternoon – two days after school broke up and just a few days before

Christmas. Mandy had also rung the Welford Parish Council offices before closing time to make sure that the hall would be available on that date. The council official thought the idea was wonderful, especially as her elderly parents and their ageing bulldog would be amongst the guests. Mandy had to make the official promise not to say a word to anyone. 'Everyone must think they're just bringing their pets along for a free check-up,' she stressed.

When Mandy told her parents about her idea, Mr and Mrs Hope readily agreed to do the vet checks and said they'd ensure Jean didn't schedule any appointments at the surgery until later on Friday evening.

'What a lovely surprise it will be for all our elderly friends,' said Emily Hope, smiling at Mandy and James. 'I *knew* you two would come up with a good idea to cheer them all up.'

The pets lucky dip took place at school during break the next day. Mandy and James's friends were delighted to join in the fun and congregated excitedly in the playground, keen to find out which pet they'd be sponsoring.

'So who's choosing first?' asked Mandy. She held out a woolly hat that contained numerous folded pieces of paper, bearing the names of all the pets belonging to the elderly people from Welford and its surrounding area.

'Seeing as it was your idea, why don't you have the first go, Mandy?' suggested James.

Mandy plunged her hand into the hat and brought out a scrap of paper. She unfolded it, read the name of the pet, then cried out, 'You'll never guess who I've got!'

'Who?' asked everyone, trying to peer over Mandy's shoulder to see the name of the animal.

'It's fat, spoilt and its name starts with a P,' announced Mandy to the excited group.

'Pandora! That has to be Pandora,' cried one or two voices.

Pandora was a Pekinese owned by Mrs Ponsonby, a large, bossy woman who fussed over her animals as if they were delicate pieces of china.

Mandy roared with laughter until tears were streaming down her cheeks, then she held out the hat to James. 'Your turn now. I hope you get Mrs Ponsonby's puppy!'

But James didn't get Toby, the mongrel puppy. His pet was Patch, the grey kitten that belonged to the shy and eccentric spinster twins, Joan and Marjorie Spry. Mandy passed the hat round and there was further laughter and delight as pets' names were read out.

'I've got Mr Bell's squirrel, Sammy,' announced Sara Bailey.

'That's just *perfect*,' said Mandy. 'You should know *exactly* what to get for him.'

'Why?' asked Sara, looking a bit perplexed.

'Because he's a rodent – just like your mouse, Muffin!' teased Mandy.

A loud yell from Richard Tanner drew everyone's attention. 'I've got Mrs Ponsonby's Toby,' he howled in amusement. 'Perhaps I'll buy him some cotton wool for Mrs Ponsonby to wrap him up in!' he joked.

The group of classmates burst into laughter again then, once the hilarity had subsided, they began to discuss their ideas for gifts for the pets.

'I'm going to knit a little blanket for Tiddles,' said Harriet Ruck, who had drawn out Ernie Bell's kitten. Harriet's father owned a flock of

Wensleydale sheep that were used for wool production.

'She'll love that,' said Mandy, looking at her watch. Break was nearly over and there was still one more aspect of the party to arrange with her classmates. She cleared her throat loudly to get everyone's attention again. 'Listen, everyone. There's one other thing,' she announced. 'The hall will need decorating, but there's no way we can afford to buy fancy decorations; that would use up all of our pocket money.' There were murmurs of agreement from the little crowd. 'But,' Mandy continued, 'if we can get enough holly, ivy and mistletoe, and even some leftover tinsel and stuff, I think we can make the hall look quite Christmassy.'

Everyone promised to scout around in their gardens and the nearby woods and fields to see what greenery they could find. Some of the classmates said they would ask their parents for any spare bits of Christmas trimmings that might be lying about their homes.

'We'll need a central collection point,' suggested James. 'I don't think Mum and Dad will mind if the shed in our garden was the depot,' he said.

'But they'll probably prefer it if you all came on just one day – like next Saturday – so that there's not too much coming and going.'

The bell rang to signal the end of break. As everyone filed back into their classrooms, Mandy turned to James. 'It's going to be a great party,' she said happily. 'I can hardly wait for next Friday.'

Three

Great, thought Mandy leaping out of bed early on Saturday morning. *No school today so we'll be able to get loads done for the party*. James was coming over to Animal Ark after breakfast and the first thing on their agenda was to cycle up the lane to Lilac Cottage where Mandy's grandparents lived. Mandy's grandad had a small holly bush in the garden and he had promised to let them have a few sprigs from it. He had also hinted that he might have an old artificial Christmas tree stashed away in the attic.

Mandy drew back the curtains and was

confronted with a white glare from the garden. A heavy frost lay on the ground. *I hope this doesn't stop everyone from going out to find mistletoe and stuff,* she thought to herself. She quickly dressed, cleaned her teeth and made her bed, then clattered downstairs, passing Emily Hope who was on her way back upstairs with a tray of tea. 'Morning, Mum,' she said as she shot past her and into the kitchen.

'Morning,' called Mrs Hope. 'I see you're in your usual Saturday morning rush!'

'James and I've got heaps to do today,' Mandy called back. 'We're sorting out all the decorations for the hall and making the invitations.'

She hurriedly ate breakfast, then went through to the residential unit to see to Biddy before James arrived. The collie dog was responding well to the acupuncture treatment, and Mrs Hope had said that Mandy could take her out to the back garden for a few minutes every day at mealtimes. Mandy prepared a bowl of food for Biddy and put it in the compound, then she fetched the dog who snuffled inquisitively amongst the bushes for a few minutes before getting stuck into her meal. Mandy left her to enjoy her breakfast and went back in to sweep out her cage and replace the bedding.

'There,' she said, returning to Biddy five minutes later. 'All clean and comfortable again.' She took the collie back indoors. 'And nice and warm in here too,' she said as Biddy settled down contentedly on the freshly laundered bedding.

A loud, excited bark outside announced the arrival of James and Blackie. Mandy grabbed the gloves and anorak that she'd left on a chair in the residential unit and ran out to meet her friend.

'I'll just get my bike,' she called.

Mandy wheeled her bike out of the shed and fastened on her crash helmet, then the two friends cycled up the lane towards Lilac Cottage with Blackie bounding along between them.

'Careful, Blackie,' shouted Mandy, as the big black Labrador leaped exuberantly into a puddle then bumped into her bike, causing it to wobble precariously. Blackie looked up at Mandy, his mouth wide open and pink tongue hanging out, as if he was laughing at her. 'You cheeky boy,' she scolded him affectionately.

'Come on, Blackie, heel,' said James firmly, but the Labrador ignored him entirely and hurtled off to splash in another puddle at the side of the lane.

'Don't say it, Mandy,' said James, seeing her grinning at him. 'I *know* he's out of control!'

At Lilac Cottage, Mandy's grandfather was inspecting his vegetable garden for signs of frost damage. 'Just as well I've only got sprouts on the go right now,' he muttered, as Mandy and James walked along the rows of Brussels sprouts with him. 'This frost would have killed anything else. Now, let me see, it's holly you two are after, isn't it?'

'Yes, please, Grandad,' said Mandy.

'With lots of berries on, please,' added James, who was holding Blackie firmly by the collar to prevent him from causing his own brand of damage to the garden.

Grandad led the way to a small holly bush at the back of the cottage. Using a pair of sharp secateurs, he snipped off a few choice branches that bore heavy clusters of the bright red berries. 'You'll need a bag or something to put them in,' he said. 'Let's go indoors and see if Gran has something you can use.'

They found Gran bustling about the kitchen,

steeped in the aroma of delicious Christmas baking. Mince pies, shortbread and chocolate biscuits lay on wire cooling racks all over the worktops. The sight made Mandy's mouth water.

'Wow, it's just like a bakery in here,' said James, ogling the bountiful spread before him.

Gran laughed. 'I suppose it is, really. You see, I've been doing some extra baking as my contribution to the party.'

Mandy was delighted. She flung her arms round her grandmother and hugged her tightly. 'I must have the best grandparents in the whole world,' she said happily.

'Perhaps I'll get a hug like that, too, if I bring in the tree,' chuckled Grandad. He disappeared into the back room and returned a moment later with a tall, but very tatty, artificial pine tree. 'It's seen better days, I know,' he told them, 'but you might be able to do something with it.'

Mandy looked sceptically at the tree. She wasn't sure that anything could be done to resurrect it, but James seemed to think otherwise. 'I think we can dress it up and make it look pretty good,' he said confidently. 'Let's tie it to my bike. I'll take it

home and work on it over the next few days.'
Mandy tried to imagine what James had in mind,
but she couldn't see any future for the battered
old tree other than in the bin!

Gran found a large plastic carrier bag for the
holly and Mandy hooked it over the handlebars
of her bike. Then Grandad helped them to lash
the tree to the crossbar of James's bike with some
gardening twine. 'Careful how you go,' he called
after them as they rode back down the lane with
Blackie running in front of them.

When they reached the Hunters' house, Mandy and James untied the tree and put it in the shed along with the other items that had been brought in so far.

'Not very much, is it?' sighed Mandy as they surveyed the little pile of trimmings that lay before them. It looked as if the frosty conditions were preventing their school friends from going outdoors to collect greenery, just as Mandy had feared earlier that morning. She began to worry that, far from looking festive, the hall would be very bare on the day of the party. 'We've just *got* to find some more stuff,' she said to James.

James took an empty cardboard box down from a shelf and began packing the greenery into it. 'Maybe more will turn up later,' he suggested.

'It'll have to be a lot more,' said Mandy. She upturned the carrier bag and shook Grandad's holly into the box.

'Why the long faces?' asked James's father, coming in to the shed just then.

'Well, we're not having much luck with the decorations,' said James. 'We'd banked on getting lots of holly and stuff to put around the hall. But so far, this is all that's come in,' he said, pointing despondently to the few pieces of mistletoe and holly that didn't even half-fill the box.

'Mmm, I see what you mean,' agreed Mr Hunter. 'And that tree's not going to win any prizes either!'

'But it's got *potential*,' protested James. Mandy smiled. James was getting quite protective of the battered old thing.

'Look, I've got an idea,' Mr Hunter said. 'After lunch I'm going up to Penell's Garden Centre to get some things for the greenhouse. Why don't you come along and see if Mr Penell has any bits left over from all the mistletoe and holly wreaths he's selling?'

Mandy and James thought it was worth a try and decided to spend the rest of the morning making the invitations, so they could deliver them the next day.

They went up to James's room and he booted up his computer. 'What should they say?' he asked.

'Ummm, what about: "You are invited to bring your pet for a free Christmas veterinary check-up. Venue – Welford Village Hall; Date – Friday 22 December. Time – 3.00 pm onwards. R.S.V.P. Animal Ark – Telephone 703267",' suggested

Mandy, sitting alongside James and watching as he began to tap away at the keyboard.

'I think there are some pictures of dogs and cats in this folder,' he said, clicking the mouse on the word *Insert*. 'We could put one or two on the invitation.'

By the time lunch was ready, the invitations were complete.

'They look really great,' said Mandy, congratulating James on his expertise, as she popped the last invitation into an envelope. 'I just hope we'll be able to get the hall looking as good.'

There was barely enough space to park a bicycle, let alone a car, when Mr Hunter turned into the carpark at Penell's, later that afternoon.

'Look, there!' exclaimed Mandy, pointing to a big banner that was strung across the entrance to the main building. '*That*'s why it's so crowded!'

'Santa's Grotto. Opening 2 pm Saturday 16 December,' James read aloud.

'That means everyone in Welford under about the age of seven will be here,' chuckled Mandy, as they squeezed through the crowds on their way to find Mr Penell.

A long queue had formed outside the grotto and Mandy recognised several of the excited young children who stood waiting for their turn to see Santa to tell him their Christmas dreams. She remembered sitting on Santa's knee in that same grotto when she was just four years old, and asking him if he'd give her one of his old reindeer that he wasn't using any more!

Halfway down the queue, a girl was waving to them. 'There's Sara Bailey's little sister, Jessie,' said James, waving back at her. 'I wonder if Sara's here too?'

Mandy glanced around and noticed Sara standing to one side. 'She's over there – next to those bales of straw. And look – she's got a cage with her.'

A small cage rested on top of one of the straw bales. Mandy could see a little exercise wheel in the middle of the cage and a big heap of shredded newspaper in one corner.

'It must be Muffin's cage,' guessed James. 'Let's ask Sara if we can meet her.'

'Hi there,' said Sara, as Mandy and James came over to her. 'Don't tell me you're waiting to see Santa!' she joked.

'No, but we *are* waiting to see Muffin,' laughed Mandy. 'I suppose she is in here somewhere.' She peered into the cage. The floor was lined with clean sawdust and in the corner there was a tiny dish containing oat flakes and seed, and a water bottle was attached to the bars. But there was no sign of a white mouse.

'She's in there all right,' Sara said, 'but you'll be lucky to catch even a glimpse of her. She's ever so shy. She just hides in her bedding most of the time.'

Mandy thought Sara sounded a little disappointed by her mouse's rather unsociable behaviour. 'Perhaps it's because she's still settling in,' she suggested, trying to make the younger girl feel a bit better about her new pet.

Sara shrugged her shoulders and was about to answer Mandy, when James, who was bending down and staring hard into the newspaper, said, 'If she's so shy, the noise and crowds in here must be really frightening for her.' As he spoke, his glasses slipped down to the end of his nose. He straightened up and pushed them back up again. 'Wouldn't it have been better to leave her at home?' he asked Sara earnestly.

'Oh, I would *never* have brought her in here if I didn't have to,' Sara reassured James. 'But it's much too cold for her to stay in the car outside.'

'But why did you bring her out in the car in the first place?' asked Mandy, puzzled. After all, Sara hadn't wanted to take Muffin to school because of the cold.

Sara explained that she'd thought Muffin seemed a bit quiet when she first got her, but assumed she'd come out of her shell after a few days. But as the days passed, the little white mouse had become even more subdued. Sara had begun to worry that there might be something wrong with her. 'Mum said we should take her to your mum and dad, Mandy, to have her checked out,' she explained. 'We were on our way to Animal Ark this afternoon but when we were driving past here, Jessie saw that Santa's Grotto was open. She begged Mum to let her go in, so that's why I'm sitting here with Muffin.' She looked at the queue snaking its way towards the grotto. 'I just hope we get to Animal Ark before the end of surgery,' she said anxiously.

Mandy glanced across to where Jessie stood in

the queue. The little girl had hardly moved forward since they'd first seen her. Mandy turned back to Sara. 'Don't worry, there's an evening surgery tonight so you've got plenty of time,' she reassured her.

Sara seemed relieved. 'If Muffin *is* sick or anything, then I want her to be treated straight away so that she's fit and healthy in time for Christmas.'

'Well, Mandy's parents are brilliant vets,' James enthused. 'They'll have her charging round in that exercise wheel in no time!'

'Do you really think so?' asked Sara, biting her lip. 'You know, I've had her for a week already and I haven't even been able to hold her yet. And I've tried all sorts of things to tame her.'

Mandy felt really sorry for Sara. She thought it must be very tough to have a pet that didn't respond to you. *I hope Mum and Dad can find out what's wrong with Muffin*, she thought to herself. *Otherwise Sara's in for a disappointing Christmas.*

Thinking of Christmas suddenly made Mandy remember why they'd come to Penell's in the first place. She looked across to the checkout counter and saw Mr Hunter waiting to pay for his purchases.

'James,' she said, tugging at his sleeve. 'Your dad's nearly finished, and we haven't even found Mr Penell yet.'

'Oops!' said James. 'We'd better hurry up. I wonder where we'll find him?'

'Why do you want Mr Penell?' asked Sara.

James quickly explained about the decorations.

'I think he's in his office,' Sara said. 'I saw him going that way about five minutes ago.'

Mandy took one more close look at the wad of bedding in the cage. 'We know you're in there, little mouse,' she whispered. 'You can't hide for ever!' Then, turning to Sara, she said, 'We'll probably see you at Animal Ark later on. Muffin will *have* to show herself then, because Mum or Dad will need to take her out to examine her.'

Sara smiled. 'I really want you to meet her,' she said. 'She's very cute. I know you'll like her.'

As Mandy and James made their way through the crowds again, Mandy glanced back at Sara. A group of small boys had gathered round her and some were poking their fingers through the bars of Muffin's cage. One boy even began to fiddle with the cage-door. In a flash, Sara lifted the cage off the straw bale, put it on her lap, and leaned protectively over it. Mandy felt a surge of compassion for her. *The sooner she gets Muffin out of here and up to Animal Ark, the better*, she thought.

Four

Mr Penell's office was up a steep flight of steps.
The door was slightly ajar, and James tapped
politely on it. After a moment Mr Penell called
out, 'Come in.'

Mandy and James pushed open the door and
found themselves in a glass-fronted room that
overlooked the entire indoor section of the
garden centre. Mr Penell stood observing the
throng in his shop below while speaking on the
telephone. He covered the mouthpiece briefly
with one hand and said, 'Hello, Mandy and James
– be with you in a minute,' then continued with

his conversation. 'When can you deliver them?' he said to the person at the other end of the phone. He listened to the reply then exclaimed, 'Not until Tuesday!' He paused, then went on, 'Oh well, it'll have to do. I think I'd better have about six or seven dozen.'

While Mr Penell was talking, Mandy and James went over to the window. 'Great view!' whispered James to Mandy. 'You can see everything that's going on down there. Look, there's Sara.' They waved at her but Sara didn't see them. She was too busy guarding the cage against the host of small children crowding around her.

Mr Penell finished his conversation and replaced the telephone on its hook. 'I've never known such a busy Christmas,' he remarked. 'We keep running out of things. Yesterday it was potted poinsettias and today we're almost out of Christmas wreaths. We're having to make some more so I've just ordered a lot of silver bows.'

'*Silver* bows?' James echoed questioningly.

'Yes, silver's all the rage this year, for some reason,' explained Mr Penell. 'Anyway, how can I help you two?' he asked.

Mandy told him about the party and their

predicament over the decorations.

'Dad needed to come here to get a load of things for the garden,' James quickly added, 'so we thought we'd see if you had anything you could let us have for the party.'

'Things like leftover bits of holly and mistletoe,' Mandy explained further.

'Any little bits you don't want will be a big help,' added James. 'We'll make use of *anything*.'

While James was speaking, Mandy looked down again at the crowds below. Sara wasn't sitting on the straw bale any more. Mandy glanced around and saw her walking quickly towards her sister and mother in the grotto queue. *She must have got fed up with all those kids trying to have a look at Muffin*, thought Mandy.

'I'm sure I'll be able to come up with a lot of bits and pieces,' Mr Penell said confidently. 'There's always some waste when we make wreaths. But I tell you what, why don't you wait until Friday morning – you'll be off school then, won't you?' Mandy and James nodded. 'By then, with Christmas being only three days away, most people will have bought their decorations, so I'll have a good idea of what I can let you have.'

'That'll be perfect. Thanks so much,' said Mandy appreciatively. 'Oh hello!' she exclaimed, as a large and very striking tabby cat with a white face and chest sauntered through the door. The cat casually brushed past her legs then jumped on to a chair next to the radiator, where he busily set about cleaning himself.

'You're gorgeous!' exclaimed Mandy, going over to pet the cat.

'Let me introduce Mungo to you,' said Mr Penell in a tone of mock grandeur. 'And I agree, young lady, he's a handsome lad, all right,' he added proudly.

'He looks pretty tough to me,' said James. He rubbed the top of Mungo's majestic head and the big cat began to purr loudly.

'He is now,' said Mr Penell. 'But he wasn't tough when I found him.'

'*Found* him?' asked Mandy. She loved to hear stories of stray animals being given good homes.

'Uh-huh, right here in the centre, when he was just a mite,' Mr Penell told them, cupping one hand to demonstrate how small Mungo had been. 'He was crouching, terrified out of his wits, behind some bags of compost. I don't know where he came from but he was as wild as a storm on the moors. It took me a long time to win his confidence.'

'He definitely looks confident now,' said Mandy, gently caressing the tomcat who had finished his grooming and was now purring contentedly.

Mr Penell smiled. 'You're not wrong there. In fact, you'd think he owns this place, the way he patrols about like a security guard. No self-respecting rat dares show his face around here!'

Mandy grinned. She had visions of Mungo strutting about while hordes of alarmed rats scurried off to safer, undefended places.

The two friends said goodbye to Mr Penell, saying they'd see him early on Friday morning, and hurried out to the carpark where Mr Hunter was loading his purchases into the back of the car.

'Have any luck?' he asked, as he pulled down the lid of the boot.

'It looks like it,' answered James. He climbed into the front passenger seat next to his father, and repeated the conversation they'd had with Mr Penell. Mr Hunter started up the engine, then turned to Mandy in the back. 'Do you want me to drop you at home?' he asked her.

'Yes please,' said Mandy. 'Sara's bringing her mouse to have a check-up and I want to be there when they arrive.'

'Can I come too?' asked James eagerly.

'Of course,' said Mandy, 'if your dad says it's OK.'

Mr Hunter agreed to have a cup of tea at Animal Ark, so that James could also meet Muffin.

'I'll collect my bike tomorrow morning,' said Mandy, remembering that she'd left it at the Hunters' house. 'Then we can ride around the village delivering all the invitations,' she added.

The waiting-room was full of people and their assorted pets when Mandy, James and Mr Hunter arrived at Animal Ark. Jean Knox, the receptionist, was looking a bit flustered. 'I think everyone wants to make sure their pets are in good shape for Christmas,' she said, consulting the blue appointments book in front of her.

'Well, there's another one coming in for that a bit later,' Mandy said. She told Jean all about Sara and Muffin.

'Mmm, in that case, I'd better make out a patient's card for Muffin,' said Jean, opening her desk drawer and pulling out a new record card.

Mandy asked Jean to let them know when Sara arrived, then she, James and Mr Hunter went through to the kitchen of the Hopes' cottage, where they found Emily Hope relaxing over a pot of tea. She was taking a short break after being on duty for most of the day.

'A mouse,' said Mrs Hope when Mandy told her about Sara and Muffin. 'I should have guessed we'd get a mouse in after the sort of day we've had today,' she joked, as she poured out a cup of tea for Mr Hunter.

'What sort of day *have* you had?' asked Mandy, taking a bottle of orange squash down from the cupboard.

Mrs Hope stifled a yawn and pushed a few strands of hair off her forehead. 'We've seen just about every type of pet you can imagine – from ponies and pot-bellied piglets to budgies and parrots and even some goldfish. Until now, though, no mouse.' She smiled. 'But Sara's going to put that right!'

A few minutes later, Jean popped her head

round the corner and told them that Sara, Jessie and Mrs Bailey had arrived. Mandy and James went back into the waiting-room just as Mr Hope was handing the previous patient's record card back to Jean. He greeted the three Baileys, then bent down and looked into Muffin's cage. 'Who have we got here?' he asked

'This is my mouse, Muffin – or rather, Muffin's somewhere in here,' Sara corrected herself, and pointed to the heap of newspaper. 'And that's the problem. She won't come out – she just hides all the time,' she added sadly.

'Ah, a shy mouse,' said Mr Hope. 'Come on in and let's have a look at her.' He picked up the cage from Sara's lap and ushered the Baileys towards the consulting room.

'Can James and I come in too?' Mandy called after them. She didn't want to miss out on this opportunity to meet Muffin.

'Of course you can,' said Mr Hope.

Inside the consulting room, Mr Hope put the cage on top of the stainless steel examination table. Simon, the practice nurse, was washing his hands in the basin in the corner of the room. He turned and looked at the cage. 'A mouse?' he asked, shaking his hands dry. Sara nodded.

'An unsociable one,' commented Mr Hope. He looked at Sara. 'Before I have a look at her, I need to ask you a few questions.'

Sara nodded. 'OK.'

'First of all,' said Mr Hope, pointing to the dish of oats and seeds in the cage, 'is she eating properly?'

'Yes. Usually the food's all gone in the morning,' said Sara. 'And I did see her nibbling at a seed earlier today. But then she spotted me and ran back into her paper nest,' she added.

'Well, if she's eating normally that's a good sign,' Mr Hope said cheerfully. 'And what about taming her? Have you done anything to get her accustomed to you?'

Sara explained that she'd read a book about keeping mice as pets and had followed the advice on taming them, but with no luck. 'She won't even take food from my hand. It's as if she wants nothing to do with me,' she said miserably.

'Mmm, it certainly seems that way,' agreed Mr Hope. 'It doesn't sound to me as if she's ill, though, seeing as she's eating regularly. But let me make sure. Can you get her out?' he asked

Sara, moving aside so that she could get to the cage.

Sara opened the cage-door and reached into the newspaper. Mandy and James had been standing to one side away from the table so as not to get in the way, but now they edged a little closer. Mandy could hardly wait to see Muffin. She'd been hearing about the little creature for long enough!

Sara rummaged around in the paper for a few seconds. 'I can't feel her,' she said a little anxiously. She probed the bedding a little longer. Then her face took on a very worried expression. She looked at Mr Hope. 'I don't think she's in there,' she cried.

Simon gently moved Sara aside and put his hand in the cage. 'Perhaps she's side-stepping your hand each time you get near to her,' he said kindly. 'As she's so shy, she's bound to be reluctant to come out in front of all of us. Let me try to get her.'

Simon picked up the heap of newspaper and drew it carefully out of the cage. He put it on the table and cautiously sorted through it, while everyone watched in silence. But there was no sign of Muffin.

For a moment, Sara stared into the empty cage, then she turned to her mother and burst into tears. 'Oh, Mum, she's gone!' she sobbed.

Mrs Bailey put an arm round Sara's shoulders. 'But where on earth could she have gone?' she asked.

'She must have escaped,' wailed Sara. She moved out of Mrs Bailey's embrace and put her face in her hands.

Mandy remembered the crowds of young children she'd seen clustering round Muffin's cage at the garden centre. A horrible thought came to her. Perhaps one of the children had opened the gate and Muffin had slipped out when no one was looking! Then, as if she'd read Mandy's thoughts, Sara looked up and blurted out, 'I bet it was one of those boys.'

'Which boys, Sara?' asked her mum.

Sara haltingly told them about the crowds of children who'd wanted to see Muffin when they were at Penell's. 'Some boys even wanted me to get Muffin out of the cage, but I wouldn't,' she explained.

Mandy looked anxiously at Sara. 'I saw those boys,' she said.

'Was that before Mungo came into the office?' asked James slowly.

Mandy shot James a look of sheer alarm. 'Oh dear,' she gasped, 'I'd forgotten about Mungo!'

'Who's Mungo?' asked Sara, drying her eyes with a wad of tissues that Simon passed to her.

Mandy looked at her father and Simon and winced. Then, putting her arm round Sara's shoulders, she said apologetically, 'He's Mr Penell's tomcat. He lives at the garden centre.'

The news of Mungo seemed to send shockwaves

through Sara. She buried her face in her hands once more and sobbed uncontrollably. Mandy didn't know what she could say to console her. After all, the situation *was* rather dire. A small, defenceless, white mouse was on the loose in the domain of a powerful rat-catching cat. The odds were definitely against Muffin!

Five

'Let's not jump to any hasty conclusions,' said Adam Hope sympathetically. 'After all, from what you've told us, Sara, no one actually *saw* Muffin in her cage at Penell's. Are you sure she was in there when you left home?'

Sara nodded.

'And I even saw her nose sticking out of the newspaper when we were in the car,' added Jessie.

There was a moment of silence. Everyone stood with lowered heads staring at the floor. It seemed that no one could think of what to do next.

Finally, Mandy broke the silence. 'Why

don't we phone Mr Penell and tell him what's happened?' she suggested, picking up the telephone directory and looking up the number for the garden centre.

'Then he can be on the look-out for Muffin,' added James, 'and maybe even keep Mungo in the office until someone finds her,' he said positively.

'Good idea,' said Mandy as she reached for the telephone on her father's desk.

At the mention of the tomcat Sara shuddered again. Mandy hoped that it wasn't already too late for Mungo to be confined. She dialled the number. The telephone rang for what seemed like ages. 'I hope Mr Penell hasn't gone home yet,' she said apprehensively, and looked at her watch. It was nearly seven o'clock. The garden centre would have been closed for almost an hour.

Eventually Mr Penell answered – he'd been locking away the day's takings in the wall safe – and Mandy told him about Muffin. When she put the phone down she turned to the others and said, 'Well, no one there has spotted a mouse yet.' Sara bit her lip. 'But the good news,' Mandy continued, 'is that Mungo hasn't moved from the office since we saw him earlier. He's been asleep the whole time. Mr Penell said he'd keep the door closed until he leaves and then he's going to take Mungo home for a few days to give us a chance to find Muffin.'

There was a sigh of relief from all in the consulting room. Sara brightened up a little. 'Let's go back and search now,' she urged her mum.

But Mrs Bailey shook her head and said, 'I don't think that's very practical, love. Mr Penell has probably locked up by now and will soon be on his way home. I'll take you over first thing in the morning. Penell's is open on a Sunday. If Muffin *is* inside the store, she should be quite safe there for the night.'

'Especially now that Mungo's not going to be there,' Mandy reminded Sara.

Sara reluctantly agreed that the search should be put off until the morning and Mandy and James promised to be at the garden centre early to help her find her pet.

'I'll come to your house straight after breakfast for my bike,' Mandy told James. 'Then we can ride up to Penell's together, and let's hope we'll get a chance to deliver the invitations straight after that.'

It was bright, but still very frosty, when Mandy set off for James's house the next morning. She had figured that their best chances of finding Muffin would be before Penell's opened and customers started pouring in, so she had phoned James before she left Animal Ark to make sure he was awake. 'We really *must* get there well before nine,' she told him firmly. James's reply was a brief grunt that Mandy recognised as a sign that she'd woken him up. *Just as well I phoned*, she thought to herself. She knew how much James hated getting up in the morning – *especially* on an icy Sunday when he'd normally have a lie-in.

A peal of bells heralded the first church service of the day and Mandy wondered briefly whether Ernie was one of the bell-ringers that morning and if he was still as gloomy about Christmas as he'd been last Monday. As she hurried past the church, she waved to a few of the congregants walking through the gate into the churchyard. Amongst them were some of the elderly folk who would be receiving invitations to the party. Mandy found herself hoping fervently that the hunt for Muffin would be successful and that she and James would still have time to deliver the invitations that day. But, more than that, she was really worried about Muffin. *She must be terrified to find herself all alone in that huge place*, she thought. Nearing the Hunters' house, she broke into a run. There was not a minute to spare.

Blackie came bounding through the door when James opened it to let Mandy in.

'*You're* certainly not joining the search party,' Mandy told the big Labrador, 'even if you *do* have a good nose for sniffing things out!' Blackie jumped up at Mandy, nearly knocking her over. 'And it's no use trying to hug me,' she laughed, pushing him down, 'you're staying home!' She looked at James. 'Are you ready?'

James had a piece of toast hanging out of his mouth and was tugging on his anorak and shoving his feet into his boots at the same time. 'Just about,' he mumbled, catching his toast with a spare hand. 'Crikey, Mandy, you didn't give me much time to even have breakfast!'

'Sara's pet mouse is in danger,' Mandy

reminded him solemnly.

They fetched their bikes from the garage and set off for Penell's. Patches of black ice lay on the roads, so the two friends had to ride cautiously to avoid skidding. A freezing wind blew into their faces as they cycled along and Mandy wished she'd wrapped a scarf round her neck.

Ahead of them, a rabbit darted across the road and disappeared into the hedgerows. 'He must be hungry to come out of his burrow into the cold,' Mandy called to James.

'And we must be heroes to come out, too,' James called back.

'It's the least we can do for an animal in need,' Mandy said.

James swerved to avoid a muddy pothole. 'You're right,' he said, as he drew up parallel to Mandy again.

They turned off the road and cycled up the driveway leading to the garden centre. Unlike yesterday, the carpark was empty.

'Oh good,' remarked Mandy. 'No shoppers yet.'

They leaned their bicycles against a wall and entered the store through the sliding glass doors. Inside they found Sara already searching for

Muffin amongst the straw bales where she'd been sitting the day before.

'You're early,' James said, wiping his glasses, which had fogged up as soon as he entered the warmth of the building.

'Mum dropped me about half an hour ago,' said Sara. 'She phoned Mr Penell at breakfast time to see if he was here yet. He was already in his office and said I could come over straight away.'

'Any clues yet?' asked Mandy, as she helped Sara to shift one of the bales to see if Muffin was hiding behind it.

'No, nothing,' said Sara dismally. 'And it's such a big place, I hardly know where to even *begin* looking for her.'

James stood silently for a moment. Mandy could see that he was working something out. 'Let's do this logically,' he announced. 'If we divide the area into three, we can fan out and each take charge of a section. Otherwise we'll just be scratching around haphazardly and won't even find an elephant, let alone a mouse.'

Sara managed to smile at James's comment. 'All right,' she agreed. 'What if I look here amongst these straw bales and all around Santa's Grotto?'

'OK,' said James. 'That leaves that big section where the plants are, which you can do, Mandy, and I'll search over there amongst the compost and fertilisers and bird seed.'

The small search party split up and moved to their respective sections. As Mandy hunted behind pot plants and trays of seedlings, she began to feel that they were searching for a needle in a haystack. *Muffin could be anywhere*, she thought, *and even if she is still in here, she probably won't stay in one place. She'll scurry off the minute anyone gets close to her, before she's even spotted, especially as she's so nervous anyway.*

The trio hunted diligently for over an hour, but to no avail. Every now and then, Mandy looked across at Sara and noticed that she was becoming more and more despondent as the search progressed without any sign of her beloved mouse. Eventually Mandy saw her sitting on a bale of straw with her head between her hands. It looked as if she'd given up hope.

Mandy went over and sat beside her. 'It's such bad luck,' she said sympathetically.

Sara lifted her head. 'I've waited ever such a long time for a pet of my own,' she said sadly.

'And now I've lost her before I even had a chance to get to know her.'

Mandy couldn't think how to comfort Sara. She didn't want to build up her hopes by saying she was confident they'd find Muffin soon, because, in her heart, she wasn't at all sure they would. Muffin had disappeared without trace.

James came over to join them. 'I was really sure I'd find her amongst the seeds,' he said. 'I mean, if I was a mouse on the loose, I'd definitely head for a good supply of food! But I *did* see something that looked like droppings.'

'*Mouse* droppings?' asked Mandy.

Sara looked eagerly at James who shrugged his shoulders. 'I don't know,' he said. 'And even if they are, how can we be sure Muffin made them? There must be wild mice and other rodents around here. Remember Mr Penell told us that Mungo is a good ra—' He stopped mid-sentence and clapped a hand across his mouth. 'Sorry, Sara,' he said, 'I shouldn't have said that.'

Sara looked away for a moment then turned back to James. 'It's OK,' she told him. 'It's no use pretending we think she's safe. You see, I don't really think she is.'

'What makes you say that?' asked Mandy trying hard to sound optimistic.

'Well, we've searched all over and haven't even spotted a whisker. And that's probably because Mungo . . .' Sarah paused and bit her lip, '. . . because Mungo caught her yesterday.'

She began to sob quietly, and Mandy put an arm round her shoulders. 'But Mungo was asleep in Mr Penell's office until he went home,' Mandy said soothingly.

'Yes, but he could have got hold of Muffin *before* he went into the office,' sobbed Sara.

Mandy knew that was true. After all, nobody could tell exactly when Muffin got out of the cage. And Mandy had seen a boy fiddling with the cage door long before Mungo went up for his nap . . .

'But Mungo couldn't have found her so quickly,' said James, surveying the distance between where they sat and the steps to the office. 'When we left you yesterday, Sara, we didn't see Mungo anywhere near here – and he's the kind of cat you can't miss.'

Sara stood up and looked out of the window. 'Even if Mungo didn't get her,' she said, 'there's something else worrying me.'

Mandy and James waited expectantly for Sara to go on. She turned back to them, 'You see,' she said, 'Muffin might have escaped outdoors and if she did, she'd be dead by now.'

'Why?' asked James.

'Because she's a pet house mouse and wouldn't know how to find food or shelter, so she'd either freeze to death out there or starve,' Sara stammered.

Mandy put her hand on Sara's arm. 'Let's think positively and believe that Muffin knew better than to go out in the cold,' she said calmly.

While the three friends were discussing the plight of Muffin, the first customers of the day began entering the garden centre. Soon, there was a loud hubbub as more and more people came in and children began to queue outside Santa's Grotto. Mandy knew that there was now no point in continuing to search for Muffin. Even if the little animal *were* in the centre somewhere, she'd never come out of hiding amidst the noise and crowds. She was about to suggest to the others that they call off the search, when Mr Penell came over to them.

'Sorry I haven't been able to help you,' he said.

'There's always so much to be done before opening time. Any sign of your mouse, Sara?'

Sara looked tearfully at him. 'Nothing. I think she's dead or . . .' she hesitated, 'Mungo got her!'

Mr Penell looked embarrassed. 'Let's hope that's not the case,' he said kindly, 'and that Muffin is just having fun exploring the garden centre. Look, why don't you go home now and I'll ring you the minute I see her. I'll ask all the staff to keep an eye out for her – and I'll put a notice up on the door for the customers.'

Sara asked Mr Penell if she could ring her mum to come and fetch her, then the three friends went outside to wait in the carpark for Mrs Bailey. They stood in silence for a while. James was kicking the gravel surface of the carpark absent-mindedly, and Mandy found her eyes wandering over to the shrubs and hedges, looking for any sign of movement. Sara just sat gloomily on a fallen tree trunk and stared vacantly ahead.

This is no good, thought Mandy. *We've got to cheer Sara up somehow – especially as it's nearly Christmas.* 'I've got an idea,' she said out loud. 'Why don't we make posters advertising a missing mouse. We could give a full description of Muffin and put the posters up all over the village. Then people would know to be on the look-out for her.'

James glanced at her quizzically. She pursed her lips and looked hard back at him as if to tell him not to say anything negative. He nodded briefly.

'Great idea,' he said enthusiastically. Mandy smiled at him with relief. 'What do you think, Sara?' she asked.

Sara slid off the trunk. 'You never know,' she said, sounding a little more cheerful, 'it could work. *Someone* might have seen Muffin – if she's still alive.'

Mandy suggested that they spend the afternoon making the posters at Animal Ark and put them up on their way to and from school the next day. Sara said she'd ask her mum to drop her at Animal Ark after lunch.

'What about the invitations?' asked James.

'Oh, we can still deliver those this morning,' said Mandy.

After Mrs Bailey had collected Sara, Mandy and James set off for the Hunters' house. As they pedalled down Penell's gravel driveway, James drew up alongside Mandy and said, 'You must be mad if you think posters will help to find a mouse!'

Mandy looked across at him and frowned. 'James!' she said in exasperation. 'Of course I don't think it'll do much good. I just wanted to make Sara feel a bit better until she gets used to what's happened.'

'Sorry,' said James. 'I wasn't looking at it like that. I just thought you were being a bit optimistic.'

'Even I know that this situation is most probably a lost cause,' replied Mandy gloomily, as they came to a halt at the end of the driveway where it joined the road.

'I know, it's awful,' agreed James, looking up and down the road to see if the coast was clear. There were no cars approaching so he pushed down hard on his pedals and, as he gathered speed, called back to Mandy, 'We'd better get a move on if we want to deliver all the invitations before lunch.'

Mandy nodded silently as she caught up with James. It was hard to have to ride away from Muffin. It was almost as if she was turning her back on her. She pedalled harder, forcing thoughts of Muffin from her mind. She would just have to concentrate on organising the party.

And she hoped that making the posters would help to distract Sara for the meantime.

Six

By the end of the afternoon, Mandy, James and Sara had produced fifteen colourful posters – five each to put up around Welford the next day.

After Sara and James had gone home, Mandy went through to the residential unit where she shook out Biddy's bed and changed her water. Then she watched while the collie walked round in circles a few times, trampling the bedding underfoot, before flopping down with her head resting on her front paws. 'Comfortable now?' asked Mandy. The dog fixed her warm brown eyes on her and she stroked the top of the dog's silky head and murmured, 'You're looking better all the time. You'll soon be bounding through the woods again.'

Mandy closed Biddy's cage and went through to the reception area. *Jean won't mind if I put one of the posters on the notice-board*, she thought. Jean was quite protective over the notice-board, but Mandy felt sure that for Sara's sake she'd happily agree to the Lost Mouse poster going up. She pinned up the notice and was standing back looking at it, when her father came in.

'*There* it is,' Mandy's dad said, picking up his diary from the reception desk. 'I knew I'd left it in here somewhere.' Following Mandy's gaze, he looked at the notice-board. 'Ah, the start of another poster campaign,' he commented.

'It's a last resort really,' said Mandy.

'I know,' said Mr Hope, putting an arm around Mandy's shoulder. 'But we won't tell Sara that,' he added gently.

Mandy smiled at him. Of all the people she knew, her dad was one of the kindest and most understanding. She couldn't have wished for better parents. How fortunate she had been all those years ago when Adam and Emily Hope had adopted her as a baby, after her real mother had been killed in a car accident.

'Penny for your thoughts,' said Adam Hope.

'Oh, I was just thinking about things,' she said. Then she went on more sombrely, 'You know, Dad, I can't help wondering why Muffin was such a timid mouse. I mean, even after a whole week, she still wouldn't have anything to do with Sara. Do you think she was sick?'

Mr Hope sat down on Jean's chair. 'Probably not,' he said, swivelling round in the chair, then leaning back and lifting his feet on to the desk. Mandy grinned as she thought what Jean would say if she saw him lounging at her workstation in that way!

'You see,' Mr Hope continued, 'mice don't often get ill. Also, Muffin wasn't off her food so I doubt there was anything physically wrong with her.'

'So what could have made her so shy?' asked Mandy, sitting on the edge of the desk.

'The same as what makes some people bashful,' he answered. 'Personality.'

'Personality?' echoed Mandy curiously.

'Yes. Just like people, mice have individual temperaments,' explained Adam Hope. 'Some will hurtle around energetically, playing with everything within reach, while others prefer a quiet life, out of the limelight, as it were. It can take quite a long time for such an individual to get used to its owner.'

'That means, then, that, after a while, Muffin would have become more confident with Sara and would have let her play with her,' suggested Mandy.

'It might not have been that simple,' said Mr Hope, swinging his feet to the floor.

Mandy frowned. Mr Hope continued. 'You see, she could have been lonely.'

'She *couldn't* have been,' protested Mandy. 'Sara spent such a lot of time with her – she just didn't want to come out of her nest!'

'Having a human for company isn't always the answer for a lonely animal,' said Mr Hope, getting to his feet and stretching. 'Sometimes, an animal needs another member of its own species to keep it company. And female mice, in particular, usually prefer to have other mice – especially other females – as companions rather than being on their own.'

Mr Hope's explanation suddenly made things

very clear. The companionship of another mouse might have brought Muffin out of her shell and all the heartache could have been so easily avoided. If only Muffin had had a friend to start with!

The next morning, Mandy left for school a little earlier than normal to give herself time to put up her four remaining posters. She tacked one up on the notice-board outside the post office, another one outside the village hall, and then hurried over to the church where she pinned one on the parish notice-board. *I'll put the last one up outside the Fox and Goose*, she told herself as she neared the bus stop at the crossroads in front of the pub.

James was already waiting for the bus when Mandy arrived. 'I've just put up my last notice,' he announced, pointing towards the Fox and Goose.

'That's just where I was going to put *my* last one!' laughed Mandy. 'Now I'll have to think of somewhere else to put it after school.'

There was no sign of Sara yet and Mandy and James looked around anxiously for her.

'She'd better hurry,' said James, glancing at his watch. 'The bus will be here any minute now.'

Just as the school bus pulled up, Sara came running along the road as fast as she could.

'Just made it!' she gasped. She then went on to tell Mandy and James about how she'd been all the way up to the tennis courts to put a poster in the pavilion there. Mandy couldn't help thinking that not many people would be out playing tennis in such cold weather. But she didn't express her reservations to Sara, because she knew that Sara was really desperate and wanted to make sure that as many people as possible knew about Muffin.

'I think we've got the village pretty well covered,' said James, as the bus chugged away from the crossroads and headed for Walton.

'That means that all we can do now is wait and hope for the best,' said Mandy, looking meaningfully at James.

By the end of the next day, there had been no response at all to the posters. Muffin had already been missing three full days and Sara had finally lost hope. 'I know I'll never see her again,' she'd said to Mandy and James after school that afternoon.

This time, Mandy knew there was little point in even pretending that the mouse would be found. But at least Sara seemed to be facing the fact that her pet was not coming back. Nevertheless, after they'd got off the bus, Mandy felt a big lump rising in her throat as she watched Sara walking off forlornly in the direction of her home, where an empty cage waited as a reminder of Muffin's absence.

That night, Mandy tossed restlessly in her bed. She couldn't get Sara and Muffin out of her mind and wished there had been a happy ending to the whole episode. She kept thinking how miserable Christmas was going to be for Sara. *I expect she's looking forward to it about as much as all the old people are*, Mandy said to herself. Thinking of the old people gave Mandy an idea. She could get Sara involved in all the arrangements for the party that was now only a few days away. She figured that helping to bring good cheer to others might help Sara to feel a bit more cheerful herself. After all, Christmas was a time of giving and sharing. Pondering the meaning of Christmas, Mandy gradually relaxed and soon drifted off to sleep.

The harsh buzzing of her alarm clock woke Mandy the next morning. She struggled to open her eyes. It wasn't like her to be so tired first thing, especially when it was the last day of term. Then she remembered that she'd lain awake half the night worrying about Sara.

As she dressed, she thought of all the tasks she could give Sara to do for the party. It would probably be best to let her do the fun things, like decorating the trestle-tables and hanging up the mistletoe, which, she hoped, Mr Penell would have for them on Friday morning. With all the worry over Muffin, Mandy hadn't spent a lot of time thinking about the decorations lately. She wondered idly how James's secret Christmas tree project was going. *It would take a genius to do something with that old tree*, she thought as she pushed open the kitchen door.

Mr and Mrs Hope had finished breakfast and were already washing up. 'Morning, love,' said Emily Hope, with a concerned expression on her face. 'Are you all right?'

'I'm fine,' replied Mandy, pulling out a chair. 'I just overslept a bit, that's all.'

'Had a bad night, did you?' asked Mandy's dad.

'Yeah, not brilliant,' confessed Mandy as she reached for the jug of orange juice. 'I just feel so sorry for Sara.'

An urgent knocking on the front door interrupted the conversation. 'Sounds serious,' said Mr Hope. He dropped the washing-up sponge into the soapy water in the sink and hurried out to the hallway, saying, 'Let's hope it's nothing too terrible.'

Mandy jumped up and ran after her dad. As the rapping at the door intensified, visions of all sorts of emergencies flashed through Mandy's mind. She'd experienced hundreds of urgent cases such as Caesarean births, accidental shootings, epileptic fits and road accidents, but was always on tenterhooks whenever a new emergency came in.

Mr Hope unlocked the door and, as he swung it open, an excited figure came bursting in. It was Sara, and she was beaming from ear to ear. Mandy could hardly believe her eyes. Sara had undergone an amazing transformation! Just yesterday, she had been thoroughly dejected and now she was bubbling with happiness.

'Guess what, Mandy?' cried Sara excitedly.

'It can only be one thing!' laughed Mandy, as Sara flung her arms round her in delight.

'Mr Penell's found Muffin!' exclaimed Sara, hugging Mandy so tightly she could hardly breathe.

'That's fantastic!' cried Mandy happily. 'When did he find her?'

Sara let go of Mandy and looked at her with shining eyes. 'Late yesterday evening,' she

answered. 'I was about to have a bath after tea, when he phoned and told me he'd just caught her. She must have come out of hiding when all the customers had left. He said he was lucky to spot her before she ran off again.'

Mrs Hope had also come into the hallway. 'So, all's well that end's well,' she said when Sara had finished her account.

'Yes, a great ending to a harrowing tale,' agreed Mr Hope. He paused, then said reflectively, 'I wonder how Mr Penell actually got hold of her?'

Sara put a hand to her mouth. 'I didn't ask him that,' she said. 'I forgot.'

'Never mind,' Mrs Hope said. 'The main thing is that you've got Muffin back again.'

'Well, I haven't actually *got* her yet,' Sara told them. 'Mr Penell has put her in a strong cardboard box up in the office. Mum said she'd go and fetch her this morning while I'm at school. I can't wait for the end of the day!'

'Just as well we break up today and get to come home early,' Mandy reminded her. 'You won't have to wait too long before you see her again.' She reached for her coat, which was hanging on the coatrack on the wall. 'I can't wait to meet her.'

'Maybe you could come home with me after school,' said Sara.

'That'd be great,' said Mandy, as she pulled on her coat.

'And James,' added Sara. 'He'll have to come too. I want the whole search party to be there to meet her and to celebrate her homecoming!' she chuckled.

'Good idea,' enthused Mandy. 'Why don't we have a double celebration – for the return of Muffin and the end of term?'

As they were about to go out of the front door, Mandy had a sudden thought. 'Let's quickly phone and see if we can catch James before he leaves for school – *and* let Mrs Hunter know he'll be home late today.'

'Talking of late,' said Mr Hope, eyeing the clock in the hall, 'that's something you two will be if you don't get a move on!'

'Oops!' cried Mandy, noting the time. The bus would be pulling up at the crossroads in less than ten minutes! 'We'd better get going! Mum, will you phone James for us and tell him the plan?'

Mrs Hope reached for the telephone. 'I'll try, but he's probably already on his way to the bus stop. I expect you'll have the pleasure of breaking the news to him yourselves, but I will tell Mrs Hunter what's happening,' she said, as Mandy and Sara tore out of the door.

As they ran down the lane towards the bus stop, Mandy and Sara chatted excitedly about the return of Muffin.

'I've already cleaned out her cage, and put new sawdust on the floor, and a big pile of hay in the corner for her bed,' Sara told Mandy happily. 'And I'm going to give her some special treats to make her feel really welcome. You know, this is the very *best* day of my life.'

Mandy grinned at Sara. 'It must be!' she laughed. 'In a way, it's as if you're getting *another* early Christmas present.'

Seven

A shout of 'Hooray' erupted in Mandy's classroom when the bell rang, signalling not only the end of the school day but also the start of the Christmas holidays.

'At last – the moment you've all been waiting for!' Their teacher, Miss Potter, laughed as the cheering gave way to an excited buzz of activity. There was a general scraping back of chairs and packing away of items into bags, then a rush for the door amidst happy chattering.

'Bye, Miss Potter,' said Mandy, as she left the classroom, 'I hope you have a lovely Christmas.'

'You too, Mandy,' smiled the teacher. Then she added, 'You and all the animals you'll no doubt be encountering!'

Mandy grinned back at her, then ran off down the corridor and out into the playground to meet James and Sara. She wondered what animals she *would* encounter during the holidays. That was one of the great things about living at a veterinary surgery – you could never tell what animal you'd bump into next!

The three friends climbed on to the bus and made straight for the long seat at the back so they could all sit together. James turned and waved out of the rear window to some of his classmates as the bus started to chug slowly out of the carpark.

Mandy opened the side window and called out to Richard Tanner who was riding along the cycle path next to the road. 'See you on Friday, Richard. And don't forget your present for Toby,' she reminded him cheerfully. Everyone had promised to bring their gifts for the old people's pets on Friday morning, before the party started.

Richard shouted back, 'I'll need a truck for the big load of cotton wool I've bought!'

Mandy laughed and pulled the window shut. She turned and looked at Sara who was almost bursting with excitement. 'Come on bus, hurry up,' Sara urged.

Mandy glowed with happiness – there was so much to look forward to these holidays. At long last they'd be meeting Muffin; then there was the party the day after tomorrow, and carols by candlelight outside the Fox and Goose on Christmas Eve. And of course, there was Christmas Day itself.

The journey back to Welford seemed to take for ever, but at last the bus drew up at the crossroads. The three friends leaped off and hurried in the direction of Sara's house, with Sara almost breaking into a run. When they reached the Baileys' home, Sara kicked off her shoes and dumped her bag in the porch, then burst into the hallway shouting breathlessly, 'We're here, Mum. Have you got her? Where is she? Is she OK?'

'Slow down, Sara,' said Mrs Bailey, coming into the hall. 'You're like a whirlwind!'

'Have you put her in my room?' asked Sara, mounting the stairs two by two.

'No, I haven't,' called Mrs Bailey after her. 'She's in the sitting-room.'

Sara spun round and ran back down the stairs. Mandy and James followed her into the sitting-room where Muffin's cage took pride of place on an upturned cardboard box in front of the bay window. Sara stopped suddenly and turned to Mandy and James, 'We'd better be quiet,' she said, 'I don't want her to get a fright. You know how shy she is.'

Mandy smiled to herself. It wasn't her and James who were making all the noise!

The three friends began to tiptoe quietly across to the cage. But as they approached, to their complete surprise, Muffin suddenly dashed out from her bedding and leaped into the mouse wheel in the middle of the cage. Then she began to whizz around on it as if she didn't have a care in the world.

'Muffin!' cried Sarah. She turned to Mandy and James, 'Just look at that!' she beamed delightedly. She kneeled down on the floor and reached a finger through the bars of the cage. 'I'm *so* glad you're back, Muffin,' she said happily.

Seeing Sara at the side of her cage, the little

mouse jumped off the wheel and scurried over to investigate the outstretched finger. She sniffed all over Sara's finger with her little pink nose, then, as if she hadn't quite made out what it was, began to gently nibble the tip of it. 'That tickles,' giggled Sara and the little white mouse looked directly at her with her piercing black eyes. 'I think she recognises me,' she said triumphantly.

Mandy and James kneeled on the floor beside their friend. Muffin glanced at the two new faces peering into her world and sniffed the bars of the cage before scampering over to her dish which was filled with oat flakes, budgie seed and tiny bits of carrot. She tasted a morsel of each type of food before settling on the carrot, which she gnawed on contentedly.

'I *knew* she'd like the carrot,' said Sara. 'I cut those pieces for her before I left this morning.'

'Maybe that's why she looks so much at home already,' said James. 'She appreciates the personal touch!'

'I wonder if she'll let me hold her yet?' said Sara. Then almost immediately she added, 'No, I'd better wait a while just in case she's still a bit nervous.'

They watched Muffin for a little longer then Mandy suggested that they use the time before tea to make some decorations for the party. She was still worried that the hall could end up looking a bit bare. 'We can make some paper chains and lanterns out of old newspapers and then paint them, like we learned to in junior school,' she said.

'Now I know why I went to junior school,' joked James.

'I'll get some paper, glue and paints,' said Sara. 'We can work in the conservatory at the big table. And Muffin can come too. It's nice and warm in there in the afternoon.'

They worked busily for a couple of hours and produced a box full of colourful lanterns and chains. Sara had put Muffin's cage right in the middle of the table where they could watch her every move. The little mouse seemed perfectly content in their company and occupied herself by shredding the hay for her bed, exercising on her wheel and having the occasional snack or drink of water.

Sara watched her pet with pride. 'Isn't she cute?' she said, as Muffin ran up the little ladder that led to a small platform in one corner of the cage.

'Yes, she's very sweet,' agreed Mandy, holding up a bright red-and-green lantern she'd just finished, 'and full of beans. From what you told us the other day, I really didn't expect her to be so lively.'

'She's hardly stopped moving the whole time we've been here,' said James, who was battling with a piece of paper that had too much glue on it. The paper kept sticking to his hand and every time he pulled it off, it stuck to his other hand. 'Can you help me, please?' he said to Mandy. Laughing, she peeled off the gluey paper.

Sara handed James a wet cloth. 'You're right, you two,' she said. 'Muffin is much more energetic and confident. Perhaps she *was* sick after all, and now she's got over whatever was wrong with her.'

'Or maybe she appreciates her warm and safe environment after having to fend for herself at Penell's for a few days,' said James.

'Could be,' agreed Sara. 'But in any case, I think her little adventure has done her good somehow. She's already a lot more fun – and she's only been home for a few hours.'

*   *   *

Mandy and James left straight after afternoon tea. It would soon be getting dark and they'd promised their parents they'd be home while it was still light.

As they trudged along, a light sleet began to fall, causing the ground to become slushy and slippery. James stretched out a gloved hand to try and catch some ice but it melted as soon as it made contact with him. 'Definitely not snow,' he remarked. 'But let's hope it'll turn to snow for Christmas.'

'Oh yes, I really hope so,' said Mandy. She longed to get her sledge out again and go sliding down from the Beacon to the bottom of the hill. Thoughts of such energetic activity brought Muffin back to her mind. 'Aren't you surprised how lively Muffin is all of a sudden?' she asked James.

'A bit,' he said. 'But better that than a dead mouse.'

Mandy smiled. 'Seriously, James, I think it's odd that she's changed so much. I mean, how can a mouse take on a whole new personality after a few days?' she asked, remembering what her father had told her about mouse behaviour.

'I don't know. Maybe she's just glad to be back home,' said James, jumping over a huge puddle on the pavement.

They carried on in silence for a while. Mandy couldn't stop thinking about the mystery of the reformed Muffin. Eventually, she looked at James and said, 'Perhaps you're right. Maybe Muffin's excursion did do her some good and now she knows how lovely it is to have a warm place to sleep and all the food she wants.'

James grinned. 'Yes, her little adventure taught her what really matters in life!'

Mandy laughed, 'James Hunter! Will you *ever* learn that there's more to life than food and sleep?'

'Is there?' James teased her.

At the crossroads they parted and went their separate ways. The sleet had become heavier and Mandy quickened her pace. She arrived at Animal Ark just in time to see her mother reversing the Land-rover down the drive. Mrs Hope stopped when she saw Mandy and called to her, 'I'm just taking Biddy back to Robbie. Coming along?'

'You bet,' said Mandy. She wouldn't miss the reunion between Robbie and Biddy for anything.

She jumped into the front seat of the Land-rover then turned around to look at Biddy. The collie was sitting upright in the back seat looking very regal. Mandy laughed. 'Any minute now, she'll start waving to people along the road,' she said to her mother.

During the drive to Lamb's Wood, Mrs Hope explained that Biddy had completed her course of acupuncture treatment and that the injury had healed well. 'I just didn't want her trotting all the way home behind Robbie's bike, so I offered to drive her home. She's going to have to build up her fitness again before she can do any really strenuous exercise.'

'But will it be all right for Robbie to walk her down to the hall for the party on Friday?' asked Mandy, thinking it would be a shame if they had to miss it.

'She should already be a bit stronger by then, so I'm sure a sedate walk will do her no harm,' said Mrs Hope reassuringly.

They turned into the lane leading to Robbie's cottage, then bounced along the bumpy path, splashing through puddles that had collected in the potholes.

'Just as well we've got the Land-rover,' said Mandy. 'But at least it must be easier for Robbie to dodge the holes on his bike than if he had a car.'

Robbie was waiting for them outside his dilapidated wooden cottage. Mandy could see him straining to get a glimpse of Biddy. As soon as Mrs Hope stopped the Land-rover, Mandy leaped out and opened the back door. Biddy knew immediately that she was home. Without hesitation she jumped out and went bounding over to her owner, her fluffy tail wagging gleefully as if she was telling the whole world how glad she was to be home.

Robbie crouched down and wrapped his arms round her neck. 'It's good to have you back, girl. I've missed you no end.' Biddy licked the old man's craggy face until he had to push her away. 'That's enough, you soppy thing,' he said tenderly and the collie rolled over on to her back with her legs in the air. 'Oh, it's a tummy rub you're wanting now, is it?' laughed Robbie.

Mandy stood with her mother watching the happy scene. She took hold of one of Mrs Hope's hands and squeezed it. 'That makes two reunions

in one day,' she said, wiping away a tear that had suddenly appeared in the corner of her eye. 'Today certainly turned out to be better than we thought it would.'

Mrs Hope gave Robbie a few instructions about exercising Biddy over the next few days, then she and Mandy got back into the Land-rover. As they waved goodbye to Robbie, Mandy called to him, 'Don't forget the free check-up in the hall on Friday.'

Mandy woke up to a bright, dry day on Friday. It was just the kind of weather she'd been hoping for because she knew how much the old people hated going out in wet, slippery conditions. She had arranged to meet James and Sara in the village hall at nine o'clock so that they could get an early start with the decorations. Then they would have to go to Penell's garden centre to see what Mr Penell had kept for them. The day before, they had carried all their home-made decorations and the few bits of holly and mistletoe down to the hall and stored them in a cupboard under the stage.

The three friends arrived at the hall almost

simultaneously and parked their bikes against the wall before going inside to start work.

'I think the trestle-tables should go here along this wall,' said Mandy, pointing to the side of the hall. 'It's best to put the food out of the way of the pets.'

They dragged the tables to where Mandy had indicated, then went to another corner where they set up an examination station for the check-ups.

'So where's the famous Christmas tree?' Mandy asked James.

'Coming,' said James. 'Dad said he'd bring it down in the back of the car before lunch.'

'I can't wait to see it,' said Mandy, helping Sara to tie a bunch of mistletoe above the entrance to the hall.

There was the sound of a car drawing up outside. 'Perhaps that's your dad now,' Mandy said to James and opened the door eagerly in the hope of getting a first glimpse of the tree.

But it wasn't Mr Hunter. It was Sara's father. He came in through the door saying, 'Is Sara here?'

Before Mandy could answer, Mr Bailey caught

sight of Sara and said to her, 'I've got some interesting news for you!'

Sara went pale. 'It's not Muffin, is it?' she asked anxiously.

Mr Bailey smiled. 'Well, yes and no,' he said mysteriously. 'You see, there's been another sighting of a mouse up at Penell's – and the description fits Muffin exactly!'

Eight

For a moment, no one spoke. Then, as Mr Bailey's words sunk in, Sara exclaimed, 'But that's *impossible*! She's in her cage at home. I even held her this morning and when I put her back inside, I *know* I shut the cage door properly – I always double-check now.'

The puzzled group stood pondering the new turn of events.

'Hmm, it's all very odd,' said Mr Bailey, shaking his head. 'I've just checked the cage myself and you're right, Sara, there's definitely a mouse in there. And she wasn't just a figment of my imagination – she stood up against the bars and twitched her nose at me when I was looking in at her. I think we'd—'

But before he could go on, Sara interjected and asked, 'So I wonder whose is the mouse at Penell's?'

'Maybe it's a wild mouse that's found a way in?' suggested James.

But Mr Bailey had checked that possibility too. Mr Penell had reassured him that he had seen a black-eyed white mouse scurrying behind the bales of hay early that morning. 'He said it was no ordinary fieldmouse,' Mr Bailey told them. 'Now, I think the best thing to do—'

Again Sara interrupted him. 'Well, someone else must also have lost a pet mouse,' she said with conviction. But Mandy wasn't at all sure that Sara really believed this. She looked as confused as the rest of them.

'It doesn't add up,' said James. He scratched his head then pushed his fringe off his forehead. 'At first there was no mouse, now there are too many.'

A vague notion had begun to form in Mandy's

mind. 'That means,' she said slowly, 'that there's an imposter.'

Sara looked at her in amazement and frowned. 'But where would it have come from and how did it end up at Penell's?'

Mandy shrugged her shoulders. 'Who knows,' she answered. 'But I think we'd better ride up there and investigate.' She grabbed her jacket which she'd slung over the back of a chair when they'd arrived at the hall earlier, then turned to the others. 'Coming?' she asked.

'You bet!' said Sara. 'But hang on, Mandy, we don't have to ride all the way up there. Dad will take us, won't you, Dad – please?' she asked, turning to her dad who hadn't said anything for a while.

'That's just what I've been trying to suggest for the past five minutes but, as usual, I haven't been able to get a word in edgeways!' Mr Bailey laughed. He tossed his keys from one hand to the other and said, 'Let's go.'

'I'll stay here and hold the fort – just in case anyone arrives early. Also, everyone's going to be dropping the presents off soon,' said James.

Mandy drew in a sharp breath, 'Oh, I didn't

even think of that! Good thinking, James.'

He grinned. 'Someone's got to keep a level head around here,' he joked.

Mandy thought Mr Penell looked rather troubled when they met him inside the garden centre ten minutes later.

'Ah,' he said, 'I'm glad you could get here so soon. Let's go up to my office – it's too crowded and noisy down here for us to have a proper conversation.'

Mandy tried to work out why there was any need for a 'proper conversation'. Sara seemed to have the same thoughts too because she tugged at Mandy's sleeve to get her attention, then whispered, 'But I thought we'd come to look for the other mouse!'

They followed Mr Penell up the steep staircase to his office, where he asked them to take a seat. He cleared his throat as if to start speaking, but seemed lost for words and said nothing. For a moment there was an embarrassing silence. Mandy felt uncomfortable and was wondering if she should say something, anything, just to change the atmosphere when suddenly the silence was broken by both Mr Penell and Mr Bailey, who started to talk at the same time.

'I've got something to—' began Mr Penell, as Sara's dad leaned forward, saying, 'What is it you want—'

The two men smiled, then Mr Bailey said, 'Go on.'

Mr Penell looked straight at Sara. 'I have a confession – and an apology – to make to you,' he told her earnestly.

Sara looked perplexed. Mr Penell continued. 'The thing is, I've been keeping a little secret from you.' He took a deep breath. 'You see, the mouse you have at home isn't Muffin!'

Sara's eyes opened wide. 'Muffin's not Muffin?' she cried in disbelief.

Mr Penell shook his head slowly.

'So who is it, if it's not Muffin?' Sara blurted out.

'It's – well – um, I don't know – call her anything you like. You see, she's – er – from the – er – pet shop in Walton,' replied Mr Penell hesitantly.

Sara looked dumbfounded. She stared at Mr Penell for a moment, then turned to her father and stammered, 'But – I don't – u-understand!'

Mr Bailey touched her forearm gently and said, 'Shhh, love, I'm sure Mr Penell's going to explain everything.'

Mr Penell got up from his chair and went across to the big window overlooking the crowded floor below. He glanced down at the crush of shoppers, then turned and went on with his explanation. 'You see, when you couldn't find Muffin last Sunday, I honestly thought that Mungo must have had her. I remembered how contented he'd seemed when he came up to my office the day your mouse went missing and I came to the conclusion that he'd caught her shortly after she'd escaped.'

Mandy looked at Sara. She was sitting bolt upright in her chair as if she was frozen to the spot. Mr Penell continued. 'I felt really bad about it. I mean, I knew how much that mouse meant to you, so I thought the best thing would be to replace Muffin with a new mouse and hope you wouldn't notice the difference.'

Mandy smiled inwardly. It was virtually impossible not to spot the difference between the two mouse personalities.

Sara seemed to be finding it hard to take in

what Mr Penell was telling her. At length, she let out a big sigh and said, 'So, after all that, Muffin's still in danger.'

'Oh no, not at all,' Mr Penell quickly reassured her. 'Not from Mungo at any rate. I decided to keep him home for a bit longer just in case the real Muffin turned up.' He paused then went across to Sara. 'I hope you're not too cross with me?' he implored.

Sara looked at her father, then back to Mr Penell and said, 'No, I suppose I'm not cross. It was nice of you to think about me, and, anyway, Muffin – I mean, the new mouse – is absolutely brilliant, isn't she, Mandy?'

Mandy nodded in agreement. Sara slipped off her chair and went over to the window. 'But I *am* worried about the real Muffin – even if Mungo's not here. I mean, all sorts of things could happen to her down there,' she said, pointing nervously to the shop floor.

'Well then,' said Mr Bailey, 'we'll just have to find her before anything *does* happen to her. He stood up and started towards the door. 'You don't mind if we go down and search for her now, do you, Mr Penell?'

'Not at all,' said Mr Penell. 'In fact, I'd like to help you.'

Mandy and Sara clattered down the stairs ahead of the two men. At the bottom they stopped and looked around them. The whole place was abuzz with activity.

'We'll be lucky to get anywhere near her with all these people around,' said Sara. She seemed defeated even before the hunt had begun. 'How do we know where to even begin to start looking?'

'What about the straw bales?' proposed Mandy. 'After all, that's where Mr Penell spotted her this morning.'

The second search for Muffin began. Mr Penell and Mr Bailey lifted the heavy straw bales so that Mandy and Sara could spot Muffin if she was hiding behind any of them. At one point, Sara groaned loudly, 'It's just like the last time – there's no sign of her at all.'

'But at least this time it doesn't feel like we're looking for a needle in a haystack,' Mandy said positively. 'We know she *was* definitely here earlier so it's more like looking for a mouse in a haystack!'

After about an hour, Mandy looked anxiously at her watch and reluctantly suggested they should call off the search. The party was due to start soon and she thought she'd better get back to help James with the finishing touches.

'But I can't just leave Muffin here,' said Sara, fighting back her tears. 'Not *again*.' Then, unable to hold back the tears any longer, she started sobbing loudly.

'Come on, love,' said Mr Bailey, drawing Sara towards him. 'It's not the end of the world.' He took out a large tissue and handed it to her. 'I'll bring you back again in the morning and we can stay until we find her.'

Then Mandy had an idea. She remembered the time she and James had made mouse-houses out of old tennis balls, when they were trying to determine how many harvester fieldmice there were in different areas of the country. She wondered if they could make something similar, but something that would actually trap Muffin without harming her.

'Perhaps we can put out some bait for her and lure her into a trap – the sort that wouldn't hurt her,' she said.

'That's not a bad idea,' said Mr Penell thoughtfully. 'I could rig up a kind of humane mousetrap, which she could get into but not out of again. Or even something simple like a long tube leading into a big sack of food might do the trick. With any luck, she'll go down the tunnel and make herself at home in the sack.'

They all agreed that the idea was well worth a try – certainly better than continuing with what amounted to a game of cat and mouse all over the sprawling garden centre – and even Sara seemed to draw comfort from the prospect that Muffin could be caught very soon.

Mr Penell promised to get on with setting up a trap as soon as he got a spare moment. 'When it's done, I'll check regularly to see if Muffin's found it,' he reassured the others, as they all made their way towards the sliding glass doors at the front of the centre.

Two big Christmas wreaths displayed on a stand near the doors jolted Mandy's memory. 'Oops, I nearly forgot,' she cried, turning to Mr Penell. 'You promised to let us have some greenery to decorate the hall – and we really could do with some.'

'Just as well you reminded me,' Mr Penell said.

'I've got some stuff for you under the counter here.'

He ducked under the counter and came up with a big cardboard box full of loose bits of Christmas greenery, then he bent down again and brought out a pile of proper holly and mistletoe wreaths. Mandy gasped as he offered them to her. 'They're beautiful,' she said in astonishment. 'Are they really for us?'

Mr Penell nodded. 'I don't think I'll be selling too many more now and I know you can make good use of them.'

Mandy tried to give him a big hug, but the wreaths got in the way and she could only manage to get her arms round them! 'Thank you,' she said, taking the wreaths from Mr Penell. 'The hall will look stunning for the party.'

Mandy could hardly see over the top of the pile in her arms, so Sara relieved her of half the load and they staggered out to the car behind Mr Bailey who was carrying the box of greenery. Mr Bailey put the box on the front seat next to him and Mandy and Sara sat in the back with the wreaths on their laps, to make sure they didn't get crushed or damaged en route to the hall.

'Just as well we didn't come by bike,' said Mandy once they were on their way. 'We'd never have been able to take these wreaths back.'

'Mmm,' mumbled Sara who was almost submerged by all the mistletoe, holly, bows and ribbons. The top wreath on her stack was level with her chin and she had to hold her head up high to avoid being scratched. She looked very uncomfortable, and Mandy was about to offer to take the top wreath from her when Sara began to giggle. 'There's something tickling my neck,' she said, chuckling.

Mandy noticed a stalk of mistletoe brushing against Sara's skin. She pushed it away. 'Better?' she asked Sara.

'Umm, maybe,' replied Sara but in an instant she started giggling again. 'Ooo, no, that wasn't it. Ooo, golly! It's still tickling. Can't you see anything else here, Mandy?' she said, pointing awkwardly to one side of her neck.

Mandy looked more closely then shook her head. 'Nope, nothing there. I'll take the top one – oh, what was that?' she cried suddenly, noticing a small movement amongst the mistletoe. 'There's something in there.'

'What?' asked Sara in alarm. 'Is it a spider?'

'Didn't look like one,' said Mandy. 'Ooh, there it is again.'

A pink object stuck out briefly from the mistletoe, then, in a flash, disappeared again.

'Keep very still,' Mandy told Sara.

Sara froze. 'Please don't let it be a bug or a beetle,' she said, with a look of sheer terror on her face.

Mandy watched intently for another appearance by the mysterious passenger, and was finally rewarded by the sight of something white and furry with a set of whiskers and a twitching pink nose. Just as Mr Bailey pulled up at the village hall, Mandy reached into the mistletoe and gently pulled out the culprit. Cupping it in one hand she stretched over and presented it to Sara.

'Muffin!' cried Sara in amazement.

Nine

Sara and Muffin mirrored each other's look of astonishment. The startled little mouse stared at Sara for a brief moment then, as quick as a flash, spun round and scrambled up Mandy's arm.

'Quickly, Mandy, catch her,' cried Sara, who was too hampered by all the wreaths on her lap to be able to move her arms freely.

Reaching Mandy's shoulder, Muffin sat up on her haunches and looked nervously around as if trying to work out a good escape route. In one smooth movement, Mandy reached across and closed her hand round the little animal. 'No, you don't,' she said firmly. 'We've had enough of your pranks.'

'Phew,' said Sara with relief. 'That was close. Thanks, Mandy.'

Hearing all the commotion behind him, Mr Bailey had turned round in time to witness the near second escape of Muffin.

'Yes, that's quite enough disruption from one little mouse,' he said. 'And enough searching! Now, we'll need to find something to put her in so that she can't make another run for it.'

'What about that box?' said Mandy, gesturing to the box of greenery on the front passenger seat. 'We could tip out all the holly and stuff inside the hall, then put Muffin in it and tape up the top.'

'OK, but you two stay where you are,' said Mr Bailey. 'I'll take the greenery inside, then come back with the box.' He picked up the box. 'Hold her tightly,' he said to Mandy. Then quickly he slipped out of his door and closed it gently behind him.

Mandy could feel Muffin wriggling around beneath her hand. 'I wish I had a better hold of her,' she said.

'I tell you what,' said Sara. 'I'll try to get the wreaths off my lap, then I can take her from you and hold her with two hands.' She edged herself as close to the door as she could, then carefully slid the wreaths off her lap into the space that was now between her and Mandy. 'It's lucky we didn't put them on the seat in the first place,' she said, as she reached over with both hands so that Mandy could manoeuvre Muffin safely into her grasp.

'Mmm,' agreed Mandy, gradually opening her hand. 'We might not have noticed her because she wouldn't have tickled you, and then she'd have ended up loose in the hall!'

'And Dad and I would have gone back to search for her at Penell's. What a wild-goose chase that would have been!' exclaimed Sara, as she closed her hands round the mouse. 'There. I've got her.' She held her hands rigidly together and rested them on her lap. 'Do you know,' she said thoughtfully, 'this is the very first time I've actually held Muffin.' She peeped through the tiny gaps between her fingers, then looked at Mandy. 'But what am I going to do now?'

'What do you mean?' asked Mandy, who was

moving the wreaths from her lap on to the pile in the middle of the seat.

'Well, Muffin is my first mouse and I'm really happy to have her back. But what about the new Muffin? You see, I've grown really fond of her already,' said Sara.

Mandy lifted the last wreath off her lap. 'Are you worried your mum and dad won't let you keep both of them?'

Sara nodded. 'A bit. But if I *can* have both of them, what if they don't get on?'

'Well, let's hope the new mouse is a girl,' said Mandy. She looked out of her window and saw that Mr Bailey was returning with not only the empty box, but James too. 'Then all your problems will be over. Muffin will probably be very pleased too.'

'Why?' asked Sara.

But before Mandy could reply, Mr Bailey tapped on the car window nearest to Mandy. She wound it down. 'I'll pass the box to you, Mandy, then, Sara, you can quickly pop Muffin into it,' said Mr Bailey. They nodded and Mr Bailey opened the back door on Mandy's side and handed her the box. James peered in the window on Sara's side, squinting hard in an effort to get his first glimpse of the real Muffin.

Sara gingerly lowered Muffin into the box then let her go. 'Quickly, close the top, Mandy,' she said swiftly withdrawing her hands from the box.

Mandy deftly folded the cardboard flaps and, for the first time in nearly a week, Muffin was once again secure. 'She's got plenty of air,' Mandy reassured Sara, pointing to a few slashes in the top of the box.

James opened Sara's door. 'Mr Bailey told me the whole saga,' he said, biting off a strip of tape from the roll he'd brought out with him and sticking it across the top of the cardboard box. 'Unbelievable!' He lifted it off Sara's lap and then she and Mandy got out of the car.

A high-pitched bark arrested everyone's attention. Mandy looked down the road and, in the distance, could just make out Robbie Grimshaw and Biddy, making their way slowly towards the hall. The first party guests were about to arrive!

'Oh, golly,' cried Mandy. 'Everyone's going to be arriving soon and we're not ready yet!'

'Yes, we are,' said James, with a grin. 'It's all

done, apart from the things from Mr Penell, and they won't take long to put up.'

'Oh, James, you're a star!' said Mandy giving him a quick hug.

James blushed, then passed the boxed Muffin back to Sara. 'I'll take those wreaths in and put them up,' he said. He heaved the bulky load into his arms and hurried back into the hall.

Mandy ran after him. Now that their surprise was about to be revealed, she felt really excited, but also a little nervous. She hoped everything would go off smoothly.

James was the first to reach the front door. He pushed it open for her, and as Mandy stepped inside she got her first glimpse of the completed hall. 'Wow!' she gasped in astonished delight. For there, standing majestically in the centre of the stage, was a magnificent Christmas tree. But this was no ordinary Christmas tree. It was tall, leafless and silver! Mandy could hardly believe her eyes.

'That's not Grandad's old tree? It can't be!' she said to James, who was grinning from ear to ear. She strode up to the stage to get a closer look at the miraculously transformed tree.

James followed her. 'I told you I could do something with it,' he laughed.

Apart from a host of tiny white fairy lights that blinked off and on alternately, the tree was quite bare. But against the dark background of the stage, James's masterpiece shimmered and twinkled in the glow of the dancing lights.

'I stripped off all the tatty bits then sprayed it with some silver paint I've had for ages,' James explained. 'And Dad let me take the lights off our own tree, just for this afternoon,' he added.

Mandy looked at him in admiration. 'I take my hat off to you, James Hunter,' she smiled. 'And the presents look really great too,' she said, pointing to the big heap of gifts that James had arranged around the base of the tree.

While they were still admiring James's handiwork, Sara came to stand with them. 'Brilliant tree!' she said, before asking, 'Where's a safe place to put Muffin?'

Mandy smiled. Muffin and her welfare were obviously at the very top of Sara's priorities. While they looked around for a suitable spot for the mouse, Sara told Mandy and James that her father had gone home to phone Mr Penell to tell him he wouldn't need to make the special mousetrap. 'I told Dad you said it would be a good thing if Muffin the second was a female,' Sara told Mandy. 'So he's bringing it here for your mum and dad to tell us what it is. I hope they won't mind.'

'Of course they won't,' said Mandy, lifting Muffin's box on to a broad shelf at the back of the stage. 'There, she should be fine up there. I don't think any of the pets will be able to reach her.'

'Not unless someone brings a monkey,' James said, chuckling. 'Oh, look, your mum and dad are here, Mandy.'

Mr and Mrs Hope had come into the hall and had stationed themselves at the check-up point. Mandy left James and Sara to put up the remaining decorations and ran over to greet her parents. 'Isn't James's tree beautiful?' she said, giving them each a quick hug.

'It's pretty striking, all right,' Mr Hope said. 'He's got hidden talents, that friend of yours.'

A chorus of 'Oohs' and 'Aahs' suddenly arose in the doorway. A group of elderly people and their pets had arrived. The sight of the dazzling

Christmas tree and all the decorations in the hall had caused them to stop dead in their tracks.

James joined Mandy, and together they went over to welcome their guests. 'We hope you like the decorations,' said Mandy.

'They certainly liven up the old hall,' said Walter Pickard, resting two cat baskets next to him on the floor.

Mandy bent down and looked into the baskets. 'Hello, you lot,' she said to Walter's three cats – the two old ginger ones, Missy and Scraps, in one basket, and Tom, the black-and-white bully, in the other.

'You've gone to a lot of trouble just so we can have our animals checked,' commented Ernie Bell, whose squirrel and kitten were also in wire cat baskets.

James winked at Mandy. 'Shall we tell them?' he said.

Mandy nodded. 'Actually,' she said to the cluster of folk in front of her, 'you're not here just for a vet check – there's a bit more to it than that.'

A smattering of surprised comments answered Mandy's announcement. 'You see,' she went on, 'we're having a Christmas party too!'

'A Christmas party!' echoed the spinster twins, Joan and Marjorie Spry, in unison. 'For us?'

'Uh-huh. *And* for your pets,' explained James. 'There's a surprise for them after the check-up.'

The next half-hour was as busy as the most hectic of surgeries at Animal Ark. Mandy and James helped Mr and Mrs Hope by holding the pets they were examining, while Sara was responsible for greeting the guests and showing them to the check-up section when it was their turn.

Most of the pets seemed to be in good shape. Sometimes people were advised to have their pets' nails clipped or teeth scaled, and there were a few overweight animals who would need to shed a few pounds after Christmas.

When Mr Hope suggested to Mrs Ponsonby that her Pekinese, Pandora, shouldn't be allowed a second helping of Christmas dinner – or of *any* dinner, for that matter – she muttered 'Nonsense!', then tucked the fat dog under her arm and, with her mongrel puppy, Toby, trotting behind her on his lead, flounced off to find a seat at the front of the hall. Mr Hope winked at Mandy and she had to put her hand over her mouth to stop herself from laughing out loud.

Eventually all the pets had been checked and there was a buzz of excitement amongst the guests, who sat chatting while they waited to see what the surprise was that James had mentioned. A few puppies managed to persuade their owners to let them have a rough and tumble and Mandy and James nearly tripped over them as they crossed the hall to the stage.

Mandy cleared her throat to get everyone's attention. 'As you can see,' she said, pointing to the pile of gifts at the foot of the silver tree, 'Santa has come to Welford a few days early.' The audience laughed. 'And this year, with the help of all our classmates, he's remembered the animals,' Mandy continued. 'There's a present here for each of your pets.' She looked towards the side of the stage. 'And Santa himself is going to hand them out.'

With that, a red-robed figure appeared from the wings. Everyone cheered and clapped as Adam Hope, in the guise of Santa, made his way to the tree. 'Ho, ho, ho,' he said jovially. 'A merry Christmas to you all.' He picked up a gift and read out the name on the card. 'Tiddles. Is there a Tiddles here?'

Ernie Bell put his hand up. 'That's us,' he said, then pointed to the crate in which Tiddles was curled up comfortably.

Santa went down the stairs and over to Ernie, and handed him the brightly wrapped parcel. With a broad grin on his face, Ernie tore off the paper amidst general cries of 'Hold it up, Ernie. Let's see what Tiddles has got!' Ernie held up a beautiful little hand-knitted blanket. It was soft and fleecy with 'Tiddles' embroidered in gold thread at one end. 'It's just perfect. Perfect. Please thank whichever of your classmates made this,' he said. He smiled warmly at Mandy and she noticed that a few tears had gathered in the corners of his eyes.

The next gift was for Toby. Mandy nudged James. 'I can't wait to see this one,' she whispered to him, as her dad carried a bulky parcel over to Amelia Ponsonby. When the paper fell away, revealing the object inside, Mandy started to giggle. Just as Richard had promised, he'd given Toby a huge wad of cotton wool! For a moment Mrs Ponsonby looked confused, but then she spread out the cotton wool to find a hollow ball with a small hole in it.

'It's a boredom buster,' Mandy told James, as Mrs Ponsonby inspected the hard plastic ball.

'What is it?' asked Mrs Ponsonby, overhearing Mandy.

'Well, you fill it with little treats,' explained Mandy, 'then Toby pushes it around until a treat falls out of the hole. It's great for a rainy day because it'll keep him busy for ages.'

A smile lit up Mrs Ponsonby's face. Mandy couldn't remember the last time she'd seen her looking so pleased. 'What a wonderful idea,' she boomed.

'Better keep it away from Pandora, otherwise she'll lose her figure!' said Santa, as he went back to the tree to pick up the next gift. Mandy snorted so loudly she had to turn away until she'd regained her composure. 'You're *impossible*, Dad!' she whispered to 'Santa' who looked at her with wide eyes, then pointed to himself and mouthed, 'Me?'

One by one, the guests opened their gifts and held them up for all to see. There were soft toys and little dog jackets, dog biscuits, catnip-filled mice, packets of budgie seed, little mirrors and bells for birdcages, Frisbees and balls. Everyone was delighted with their gifts.

When the last present had been unwrapped, Santa waved goodbye and left the stage to tumultuous applause and cries of, 'Thanks, Adam, you made a wonderful Santa!'

'I didn't think we could hide who he was,' laughed James.

'No, Dad's not easy to disguise,' agreed Mandy, 'and he's a real natural at playing Santa!'

Ten

As soon as the gift-giving ceremony was over, Mandy, James and Sara positioned themselves behind the long trestle-tables and began pouring tea into the cups which James had set out earlier in the day.

'Ooh, what a lovely spread,' said Mrs McFarlane, helping herself to a few mince-pies. 'Who did all the baking?'

'Gran did most of it,' Mandy told her, 'and James's mum made the fruitcake.'

Mr Hope was next in line and as he reached for the biggest piece of cake on the table, a loud voice behind him filled the air. 'You'd better not have any seconds, Santa, or you'll get stuck in a chimney.'

Adam Hope roared with laughter, as Mrs Ponsonby wagged her finger sternly at him. Mandy was amazed. First, Mrs Ponsonby had smiled and now she was actually cracking a joke. 'I didn't know she had a sense of humour,' she whispered to James.

'Must be the Christmas spirit getting to her,' chuckled James.

The throng around the tea table soon thinned out and James was about to pour out three glasses of well-earned lemonade, when the door at the back of the hall burst open and Gran bustled in. Behind her trailed a crowd of merry pensioners.

'Let the party begin!' declared Gran cheerfully, as she led her entourage into the hall.

'Gran!' cried Mandy. 'What a surprise.' As she spoke, she made a rough mental calculation of how many people Gran had brought with her, then she looked at the few remaining items of food on the table. They were presented with a numbers problem that even James would have trouble solving!

'Don't worry, love,' said Gran, who seemed to guess exactly what Mandy was thinking. 'The W.I. has been hard at work. We've brought dozens of extra mince-pies.'

Gran then explained to Mandy and her two friends how she and the other members of the Welford Women's Institute had rounded up all the old-age pensioners in the village and virtually herded them to the hall. 'It seemed a pity for them to miss out on all the fun,' Gran said. 'Some of them were a bit reluctant to leave their tellies and the warmth of their fires, but we bullied them into coming out and now I think they're quite pleased.'

The three friends poured out more cups of tea, while Gran and some of the W.I. members piled the empty plates with fresh mince-pies. Soon all the newcomers were absorbed into the general crowd and the hall reverberated with the sound of happy laughter and chatter.

'I think it's safe for us to have our drink now,' said Mandy, reaching for the bottle of lemonade.

'Oh good, Mum and Dad are here,' Sara cried, just as Mandy was about to start pouring. 'And they've brought Muffin the second.' She beckoned to Mandy and James. 'Come on. Let's find out if it's a boy or a girl.'

Mandy put the bottle down and sighed. 'I guess the lemonade won't go off,' she smiled.

Mr Hope readily agreed to conduct the examination. Carefully he opened the cage, then grasped the mouse gently by the root of its tail and brought it out of the cage. Sara gasped when she saw how Mr Hope was handling her pet. 'This is the best way to hold mice,' Mr Hope reassured her. 'It doesn't hurt them – as long as you've got hold of the root and not the tip of the tail – and they can't escape.'

Mandy held her breath as her father held the mouse up in front of his eyes and scrutinised it closely. By now most of the people in the hall had gathered around to see what was going on.

Mrs Ponsonby was right at the back of the crowd and couldn't see what was causing all the fuss. 'What is it?' she called out loudly. 'Do let me pass,' she said, elbowing her way to the front.

'This should be good!' James said to Mandy.

Mrs Ponsonby burst through the crowd right where Adam Hope was standing, and came face to face with the mouse that was dangling from his raised hand. A shocked expression took hold of her face and for a moment she stood with her mouth wide open, unable to speak. Then she screamed, 'A rat! Oh dear, it's a rat!' and buried her face in her hands.

'It's *not* a rat,' said Sara indignantly. 'It's a harmless little mouse and it's *my* pet.'

A few giggles erupted from the crowd. Slowly Mrs Ponsonby looked up.

'See!' Sara said firmly. 'It's a sweet little mouse.'

'Humph,' grunted Mrs Ponsonby, 'but it's still a rodent!' and she pushed her way back through the crowd.

'I guess leopards don't change their spots after all,' Mandy told James. Then she turned eagerly to her father. 'So, what is it, Dad? A male or a female?' She glanced at Sara who was anxiously chewing on a fingernail.

Mr Hope returned the mouse to the cage. 'Well,' he announced, 'Muffin the second is a female – and a young one too.'

'Phew,' sighed Mr Bailey. 'No chance of a mouse population explosion. That means you can keep both mice, Sara.'

'Great,' cried Mandy and Sara.

'And because she's young,' Mr Hope went on, 'there should be no problem introducing her to Muffin. Two young females should live quite harmoniously together.'

'Oh, so *that's* what you meant, Mandy, when you said that Muffin will be pleased if this one's a girl too,' said Sara.

Mandy nodded.

'Well, let's introduce them right now,' said Sara and she dashed off to fetch the original Muffin from the shelf at the back of the stage.

A couple of puppies were still racing around the hall and Mrs Hope suggested that they be restrained until Muffin had been transferred back into her cage. 'We don't need any unfortunate accidents now,' she said.

There was absolute silence as Sara unsealed the cardboard box. Even Mrs Ponsonby was craning her neck at the back of the group so that she could watch the transfer.

'By the tail,' Mandy reminded Sara.

'I'll try,' said Sara, sounding rather unconvinced, but within a few seconds she had caught the little mouse and was holding her firmly upside down by her tail. Muffin's tiny front paws flailed around in the air, as she tried to find a firm surface to get hold of. She wore the same startled expression she'd had on her face when Mandy pulled her from out of the mistletoe earlier that day.

'If she looks surprised now, wait until she meets her new friend,' chuckled James.

Mandy opened the cage door. She could feel the tension in the air as Sara popped Muffin in through the gap. The little creature kept still for a moment, as if she was trying to reorient herself to her changed surroundings. Then she pricked up her little pink ears and twitched her nose as her new companion crept up to her. The two mice sniffed each other's quivering noses warily, then started slowly walking round in circles, the new mouse following Muffin.

'How are you ever going to tell them apart?' asked Robbie Grimshaw, shaking his head. 'I've already lost track of which one's the real Muffin.'

'Well, you can see that Muffin's a bit bigger at the moment,' said Sara. 'And she's quieter, remember.'

'She has been, up to now,' said Mr Hope. 'Anyway, don't you think we should leave them on their own for a while so they can get to know one another without the eyes of the world on them?'

Sara welcomed the suggestion. 'I'll put them back up on the shelf,' she said. 'It's nice and private there and out of harm's way.'

Mandy thought Sara looked very proud as she moved her two precious charges to their temporary refuge.

The crowd of mouse-watchers dispersed and began to form smaller huddles in different parts of the hall. Mandy noticed Mrs Ponsonby and Eileen Davy chatting intently together next to the piano. *I wonder what they're talking about*, she thought. Her curiosity was short-lived. Eileen Davy pulled out the piano stool, sat down, and ran her fingers over the keys. At the same time, Mrs Ponsonby clapped her hands together and announced loudly, 'Time for a sing-song!'

Guests clustered around the piano as Eileen played the first few bars of 'O Little Town of Bethlehem,' then Mrs Ponsonby filled her lungs with air and droned flatly, 'Above thy deep and dreamless sleep . . .' almost drowning out the music with her loud voice. For a minute, Mandy thought that Mrs Ponsonby's terrible voice would put off everyone else, but the opposite happened. By the time Eileen was playing the notes for 'Yet in thy dark streets shineth . . .', all the guests had joined in. The voices soared in harmony and now it was Mrs Ponsonby's voice that was almost drowned out.

Mr and Mrs Hope had also joined the impromptu choir and Mandy took her place alongside them. Standing next to her father, Mandy could hear his clear, strong voice ringing out in perfect pitch.

'. . . are met in thee tonight.' The carol came to

an end and there were calls of 'How about "Little Drummer Boy"?', ' "Good King Wenceslas"?', ' "Oh Come All Ye Faithful",' ' "The Holly and the Ivy",' as people begged for their favourite carols and Christmas songs to be played.

The party was now in full swing and for the next hour or two there was no let up in the festive atmosphere. Even the pets seemed to enjoy all the activity around them. Cats, budgies and squirrels looked out curiously from their baskets and cages that were safely stowed on separate shelves around the hall, while dogs and puppies played together gleefully.

Pandora looked as if she was having a particularly good time. During the singing, Mrs Ponsonby put her down on the floor. The plump Pekinese instantly changed into a vacuum cleaner and went around gobbling up all the crumbs that had dropped off people's plates. Mandy tugged at Mr Hope's sleeve and pointed to Pandora. Her father shrugged his shoulders, then leaned over and, winking at his daughter, confessed, 'A dog after my own heart.'

Mandy shook her head. 'There's no hope for either of you!'

Even the new supply of mince-pies was soon finished, but Gran amazed Mandy by bringing out yet another boxful, and Emily Hope helped Mandy to brew more tea. It wasn't long before everyone was tucking into the new round of refreshments.

'Now tell me they'd rather be at home by the fire,' chuckled Gran, as she helped Mandy and Sara to carry the used plates and cups through to the kitchen.

Mandy was feeling really pleased with the way things had worked out, but she couldn't get rid of a nagging thought at the back of her mind that, maybe, the two mice wouldn't get on. *What will happen if they don't?* she wondered to herself. She could see that Sara was also a bit worried, because she kept glancing anxiously towards the cage. But, from a distance, it was impossible to see what the two mice were doing, as it was now quite dark at the back of the stage.

As the afternoon drew to a close, people started saying their goodbyes and Mandy and James positioned themselves at the door to see their guests off.

'It's been a wonderful party,' Joan Spry said to Mandy and James.

'Mmm, lovely,' agreed her twin sister, Marjorie.

'Oh, aye, you youngsters have done a grand job,' Walter Pickard said. As he pulled on his big trench coat, he glanced up. Hanging from the doorframe above him was a bunch of mistletoe. He looked around. Standing on either side of him were the Spry twins. 'Oh, well!' he exclaimed. 'It can't be helped,' and he kissed each twin on the cheek.

Mandy and James laughed, then, as quick as lightning, James took a big leap out of the way so that he was well away from the mistletoe.

'Coward!' said Mandy.

Slowly the old folk left the hall. Some of them seemed reluctant to go, and all agreed that this was just the kind of Christmas they'd always longed for.

'It's what Christmas *should* be all about,' said Miss Davy. 'Not just sitting and watching telly, but people getting together to celebrate and share the festive time.' She hugged Mandy and James. 'Thank you for giving us all such a marvellous time – it's the best Christmas present I've had for as long as I can remember!'

A warm glow filled Mandy from head to foot. Not one of their guests had mentioned anything about not being bothered about Christmas any more! In fact, some of them had even arranged to get together for Christmas dinner. The party had been a total success. There was enough Christmas spirit in Welford now to last everyone – young and old – for years to come.

'Well, that's that,' smiled Mr Hope when the last guest had left. 'Now, let's see how Muffin and Muffin are doing,' he said.

Sara nervously led the way up the steps on to the stage, then lifted down the cage from the shelf and put it on a chair next to the Christmas tree. Everyone gathered eagerly round the cage. Flashing on and off, the lights from the tree illuminated the cage in bright bursts, giving just enough light to allow everyone to see what was going on. And what they saw caused sighs of relief all round. The two white mice were having the time of their lives. They were racing round the cage, tumbling over each other, spinning round on the wheel and chasing each other up and down the little ladder.

'They're having their own party,' chuckled James. 'It's as if they've got a good dose of Christmas spirit too!'

'What's going on now?' said Sara with concern, when one mouse grabbed hold of the other in its front paws and started nibbling the fur on its head.

'Nothing to worry about,' said Mrs Hope, releasing her long red hair from the scrunchy that had held it in place all afternoon. 'It's just a bit of grooming which tells me they've already sorted out who's who.'

Sara's face shone with delight. Then she put her chin in one hand and said, 'You know, Mr Grimshaw was right. It's going to be hard to tell them apart – Muffin isn't the Muffin she was when I got her. She's full of beans now!'

'That's just what I thought would happen,' Mandy said, 'and what I wanted to tell you earlier.'

Sara looked at her and frowned. 'Do you mean you *knew* Muffin's personality would change so much?'

'Well, I don't think it's that she's *changed* so much as that she's cheered up.' Mandy pushed a finger through the bars of the cage and immediately both mice ran over to investigate this new thing in their midst. 'You see, after Dad explained to me about female mice liking company, I realised that Muffin was probably not sick or shy as we had first thought. She was just bored and listless because she didn't have a playmate. Now that she's got a friend, she's come out of her shell.'

James smiled. 'So, we *can* say that Muffin's little outing did her the world of good after all!'

'Yes,' laughed Sara. 'If she hadn't got out, we'd never have got Muffin – I mean – er, the other mouse.'

Everyone laughed. 'You'll have to think up a name for the new one,' Mrs Bailey said.

Sara thought for a minute then announced, 'Crumpet. Her name is Crumpet.'

'Muffin and Crumpet – sweet, like their namesakes,' smiled Mr Hope.

'But you'll *have* to find some reliable way of distinguishing them, Sara,' said Mr Bailey. 'They'll soon be the same size.'

'Yes, I know,' said Sara. 'And they're almost like twins already.' She studied Muffin and Crumpet closely for a few moments.

Mandy and James peered over her shoulder, in an attempt to find one or two distinguishing features. 'Look,' said James at last. 'One of them has a tiny kink at the tip of her tail.'

'Oh yes, you're right,' said Sara. She studied the mice again then said. 'It's Crumpet. Crumpet's got the kink.'

'Well spotted, James,' said Mandy.

'Now that's sorted out,' said Mrs Hope, 'it's time to pack up. We've got to get home to start preparing for the next Christmas feast!'

Half an hour later, as the three friends packed up the last of the decorations into a cardboard box and removed the lights from the silver tree, Sara turned to Mandy and James. Sighing happily, she said, 'You know, Muffin and Crumpet are the best Christmas present anyone could *ever* have!'

Mandy grinned. 'Yes, and you didn't get just one present. Because of the mystery of the missing mouse, you've ended up with two happy pets just in time for Christmas!'